Christine's eyes blazed with anger

And she was hurt, too. "What you're thinking just isn't true," she said. "Laurie has other reasons for staying on as manager."

"Any fool can guess what they are." Kevin's tone was cool, his glance skeptical. "You're a very attractive girl, Christine. Oh, I'm willing to admit you can get everyone else around here to eat out of your hand. But not me!"

For a moment she was tempted to fling the truth into his dark, mocking face— but what was the use?

He had always believed the worst of her and a stubborn sense of pride forbade the explanation of her motives to this interfering stranger. Let him think what he pleased!

Fringe of Heaven

by

GLORIA BEVAN

Harlequin Books

TORONTO • LONDON • NEW YORK • AMSTERDAM
SYDNEY • HAMBURG • PARIS

Original hardcover edition published in 1978
by Mills & Boon Limited

ISBN 0-373-02224-7

Harlequin edition published December 1978

Printed in Canada

CHAPTER ONE

NOT even the ominous swerve of the Mini making her aware that she had collected a flat tyre on the lonely New Zealand road could quench Christine's feeling of excited anticipation. For some time she had been dropping down mile after mile as the road wound down into a ravine. Now steep rock faces rose high on either side of the highway and the intense stillness was broken only by a lilting fall of notes from a tui in a tree far above.

What matter if she did find herself alone in the ravine? Someone was bound to come to her rescue before long. She recalled the stock transporters with their long trailers of closely-packed sheep, the heavy trucks that had thundered past her on the long approach to the gorge. Back home in England she had often driven her mother's elderly car and on the rare occasions when she had found herself in need of help on the road luck had been with her. Well—a smile touched her soft lips—call it luck. She could scarcely be unaware of a slim supple figure, of fine spun gold hair and dark eyes and happily a smooth skin that tanned rather than burned in the summer sun. Not when masculine eyes were so frankly appreciative. But what was an attractive appearance when there was no one to attract? Minutes went by and when there was still no sign of any other vehicle on the road Christine decided to have a go at changing the wheel herself. She had taken the spare from the boot and had got as far as loosening wheelnuts when there was a squeal of brakes and a great logging truck pulled up beside her.

'Trouble, lady?' The Maori driver, a massive figure in black bush shirt and tattered denim shorts, was dropping down from the cab, his goodnatured face wreathed in a friendly grin.

'Just a puncture.' She was indescribably relieved to see him. Of course she had known that help would arrive before long, but all the same ... She pushed a strand of fine blonde hair back from her eyes and smiled over her shoulder. 'I'll get the jack.'

The grin on the pleasant face was wider than ever. 'What you want a jack for, lady?' To Christine's astonishment he strolled to the rear of the car, took a deep breath and lifted the Mini bodily. 'If you could shove on the wheel, miss?'

Swiftly she did as he suggested and in no time at all it seemed to her he was tightening the bolts. A swift inspection of the remaining tyres and he was back at her side. 'You'll be all right now?'

'Yes, thanks to you.'

He made light of her thanks. 'No trouble at all—going far, miss?'

'Not too far,' she said happily. 'It's a place called Te Weka, a few miles out of Gisborne. I can hardly wait to see it.'

Evidently she must have pronounced the Maori syllables correctly for he recognised the name immediately.

'You won't make Te Weka before dark.'

'I don't mind, so long as I get there!'

'You'll be right.' He climbed back into the cab of his logging truck and put the vehicle into gear. The last Christine saw of him was a large brown hand lifted in a gesture of farewell.

As she put the car into low gear in readiness for the long upward ascent the feeling of happiness surged back. Why not? There surely couldn't be many girls of twenty-one who out of the blue had been willed a property on the other side of the world. Bless you, Uncle Ben, she thought. I wish I could thank you, but perhaps you know, wherever you are, how delighted I am with my inheritance. Even if we didn't ever know each other, even if I did just happen to be your only living relative. Three hundred acres on the east coast of the North Island of New Zealand plus a house and an old abandoned hotel—it all sounded like a dream, but now that she was actually in the country, making her way along the main highway ... Christine hummed a snatch of song, she felt so happy.

On her arrival in Auckland after the long flight from London she had spent the night at a motel near the airport. In the morning she had stayed only long enough to hire a small car.

'It's a long drive down to the east coast,' the friendly girl at the hire-service desk at the airport had warned her. 'Why not stay in Rotorua for a night and take in the thermal sights? All those geysers and hot pools are well worth a visit.' Christine, however, was impatient to reach her destination and presently, armed with a map the girl had given her, a brand new fashion outfit and a lot of hope, she was guiding the Mini down the motorway and heading south. Indeed, she enjoyed the drive, especially once she was beyond the outskirts of city and suburbs and out on the main highway, passing by farmlands dotted with grazing sheep and driving through small settlements with their brightly painted timber houses, flower-bordered, and attractive modern stores.

When at length she emerged from the shadows of the gorge a purple haze bathed the surrounding hills. What odds if she didn't reach her destination until long after darkness had set in? What did anything matter today? Right at this moment even thoughts of Jason failed to dampen her high spirits. The intoxicating sense of finding herself in unfamiliar surroundings, the clear clear air, the winding road ahead, all conspired to give her a sense of independence and anticipation. Was this what falling out of love was all about? This sudden sense of freedom. Freedom to fall in love again?

A long transporter swept towards her, the sun-bronzed young driver dropping speed to keep pace with the Mini. To Christine his meaningful glance scarcely registered. She was accustomed to masculine interest and took no notice. At length the driver with a parting toot of the horn, swept past and she settled back in her seat, her eyes on the fragment of lighted road ahead, her thoughts wandering.

Come to think of it her appearance hadn't done her any great service, not really. The only serious love affair in her life had come to nothing and the awful thing about it was that she didn't even regret the loss. Once she had imagined herself to be genuinely in love with Jason, had believed without question his whispered protestations of lasting devotion. Dreadful to realise that now, only a few short months later, she didn't seem to care. Could it be that she hadn't the capacity of real, deep-down, once-in-a-lifetime loving? Was it something to do with her appearance, the fact that she attracted men so effortlessly that her life had been a succession of shallow friendships—even Jason. Or was it possible that somewhere, some day, there would come into her life a man with whom she wouldn't fall out of love, not ever? A man who would love her not merely for her beauty but *for herself?*

Funny to think that it had taken a fall at a local gymkhana to give her an insight into Jason's real feelings towards her. To make her realise that in spite of all the flowers and gifts, the intimate little dinners at expensive restaurants, the soft words and promises, he hadn't really cared. Not when the toss at the high jump that had landed her in hospital for three long months had had the effect of causing him to lose all interest in her. Why had she not realised earlier that he had always displayed a horror of sickness and hospitals? No doubt a riding accident came into that category.

Jason's first visit to the ward following her return to full consciousness had been anything but encouraging. His words on that occasion should have warned her of what was to come. She had known that he loathed horses and had no interest in shows or gymkhanas, but nothing had prepared her for the note of triumph in his voice.

'I told you this would happen. If only,' went on the smug self-satisfied tones, 'you would listen to me for a change.' Belatedly an expression of concern crossed the neat features. 'You were lucky to get out of this alive. That mare of yours you set such store by, I never did trust her!'

'It wasn't Misty's fault!' Christine had roused herself to protest. 'I don't remember anything except seeing the high fence ahead——'

'Then how do you know?'

'I just *know*. She would never let me down! She's got such a big heart, she's so proud and sure she would never make a mistake. Something must have frightened her at the last moment.'

Jason had sighed exasperatedly. 'You never learn, do you? Next time it could be a whole lot worse.'

Christine had choked down the lump in her throat and blinked away the stupid tears of weakness. She tried to ignore the hard angry light in Jason's eyes. 'I'll get over this lot first. Next time,' she had persisted stubbornly, 'I won't come off.' Even then she knew there wouldn't be a next time, not unless she could get the better of the crippling onslaught of terror that overcame her at thought of the high jumps that in the past she had taken on her beloved Misty.

The hospital doctors had told her she had lain unconscious for two weeks and had been barely aware of her surroundings for a week after that. They had assured her that the only after-effects of concussion would be an occasional headache and that would wear off in time. Just as this stupid fear of jumping would fade away. Just give her time.

As the days of convalescence crawled by Jason's calls became more and more infrequent. In the end it came as no great surprise to her when on his last visit Jason, red-faced with embarrassment, had come right out with the truth. He thought she should know ... he had met someone else, a girl who had come to work at his office. He knew Christine would understand.

Almost as if fate was bent on changing the pattern of her life-style, on the day she left hospital a letter arrived from a firm of solicitors on the other side of the world. The contents were staggering. She had been only vaguely aware of the existence of her dead father's brother who had long ago settled in New Zealand. Now it seemed he was no longer alive and Benjamin Rowles' sheep-farm on the east coast of the North Island was willed to his niece, Christine Rowles—incredibly, unbelievably herself!

'Quite an impressive inheritance,' her own solicitor told her when she consulted him at his office on the following day. 'Three thousand acres of hill country, some of it in bush, sheep, cattle, a farmhouse,' he consulted the legal document, 'and this old hotel on the property as well. However, seeing it is described here as being in an extremely bad state of repair it might already have been demolished.' The keen eyes raked her face. 'You'll want to put a manager in charge?'

'A manager?' Christine's brown eyes opened wide. 'I hadn't thought. All I know is that I want to go out there and stay for a time, see it all for myself.'

'See it by all means, but I wouldn't advise——'

Christine laughed. 'Don't worry! I know what you're thinking, but I'm not planning on trying to run a sheep station all on my own. I'll go out to New Zealand and when I get to the property I'll just play it by ear.'

'You like the country life, I take it, riding and so on?' She had told him about the riding accident.

'Oh yes, I do——' The eager tones faltered. 'At least——'

'Well then, you might decide to stay on for a few months. It will be getting on towards autumn in the southern hemisphere. You might care to join up with the local Hunt club?'

'It's an idea.' She forced her voice to an enthusiastic note. 'Why not?' If only she could banish from her mind the mental knock that assailed her whenever she thought of taking her mount over a jump. Even to imagine a low brush barrier was to invite the miasma of black terror that no amount of rationalising could shake off. The haunting fear was obscurely worrying.

Something of her attitude must have got through to him,

for he abandoned the subject, saying easily: 'According to this letter Te Weka is a small settlement some miles out of Gisborne. So if you feel inclined to take a job in the city to fill in your time while you're there you might be lucky enough to get something in your own line—fashion designing, wasn't it?'

Christine nodded. 'I might think about it.' That way there would be no need to come to grips with her own private devil, the one who raised his jeering head whenever the thought of taking a high jump on horseback flashed into her mind.

She came back to the present, realising that the solicitor was leaning back in his swivel chair, his alert eyes clouded with an expression of nostalgia. 'You'll like Gisborne,' he said thoughtfully. 'I once spent a holiday there staying with my married sister. The thing that struck me right away was how friendly everyone was; folk simply couldn't do enough for me. I soon found out that the city had a reputation for that very thing. They say it came of the place having been isolated for many years behind the high hills. That was before they cut a road through the mountains and got a plane service running to the main cities, but I guess it will be just the same friendly place today as it was then. It's something about the district, everyone goes out of their way to help you, make you feel at home.'

Christine left the solicitor's office still feeling as though she were in a daze. The one thought in her mind was that she wanted to go out to New Zealand as soon as possible. For what was there to wait for? It would be a wrench to part with her beloved Misty, but she was fortunate in being able to hand the mare over to a woman friend, a capable rider who Christine knew would take good care of the mount.

She had already given notice of resignation to the manager of the small workroom where she worked. Christine's mother, long a widow, had recently remarried, and although they had not put the matter into words Christine knew that her mother and stepfather were delaying their honeymoon trip until she herself had departed for New Zealand.

Smiling and happy they had seen her off at Heathrow airport. Could it have been only a day or two previously? So soon now she would be able to view her inheritance. She was curious about the farm house in which she would be living for the next few months, but it was the old hotel that captured her imagination. Imagine me, she thought, owner of a hotel.

As she sped on through the darkness she caught passing glimpses of small settlements that consisted of a cluster of lighted houses, a petrol pump and general stores. Then even these signs of civilisation became further and further apart.

Te Weka Hotel: a name flashed up to meet her eyes. Almost before she realised it she was past it and had to reverse back to the top of the hill. Her heart gave a leap of anticipation. There was no mistake, the name was spelled out, not exactly bold and clear but faded and barely decipherable at the top of the old building at the roadside. Sagging verandahs, dilapidated appearance, but nevertheless *her* hotel! It hadn't been pulled down after all. Far from it, for lights blazed from front windows and music, a stereo perhaps, drifted out on to the road. She would be lucky to find a parking place, she thought, guiding the small car between the trucks, Land Rovers and cars that were clustered haphazardly on the dried grass.

A short distance away she caught the dim outlines of a squarish brick house where light streamed out over a wide porch. Perhaps she had better announce herself, make herself known to the housekeeper. She felt certain that Uncle Ben, a bachelor, would employ a housekeeper to look after his home. Christine pictured a motherly soul, on the plump side, wearing a neat dark-coloured frock and crisp white apron. No doubt the housekeeper would give Christine a warm welcome. She would offer her a light meal, Christine suddenly realised how hungry she was, then over poached eggs, tea and toast they would chat together and she would hear all about Uncle Ben. His work, hobbies, the district where he lived—oh, everything!

As she stumbled over the rough ground leading to the house she regretted not having provided herself with a torch, but at last she reached a small gate. She followed a concreted path leading to a lighted verandah, then tapped on the door. There was no answer. Except for the porch the house appeared to be in darkness, so probably the housekeeper had gone next door. Christine turned and made her way towards the lighted building.

She pushed open the door, then stood motionless for a moment, blinking in the glare of light in the high-raftered room. Confusedly she became aware of a makeshift stage where two lads who had been playing a banjo and accordion were laying down their instruments. Couples standing on the dance floor turned to eye her enquiringly. To Christine it was all like a play or a nightmare. Did she imagine it, or was there hostility as well as surprise in the startled glances?

'Hello!' She paused uncertainly. *It's your own place, you own it!* she told herself fiercely in an effort to brace her sinking spirits. *I know, I know, but there must be some ghastly mistake.*

Aloud she said into the silence: 'This is Glendene, Benjamin Rowles' property at Te Weka ... isn't it?' and knew by the grinning faces of the Maori musicians that she had mispronounced the native name. The next moment she became aware of a well-built young man with thick blond hair and an anxious expression who was approaching her from the dance floor.

'You must be Christine,' he had a shy hesitant manner, 'the old man's niece?'

'That's me!' She forced a bright smile to her lips. 'Fresh out from London.'

The young man with the honest face appeared as taken aback by her appearance as she herself was at her reception. Clearly at a loss for words, at length he shot out a work-roughened hand. 'Laurie's the name, Laurie Stuart.'

He mumbled almost incoherently. 'We weren't expecting you to arrive for a week or two.'

Christine's impression of being definitely unwelcome here was strengthening with each passing moment. She realised that couples were leaving the dance floor to seat themselves on hay bales scattered around the walls of the long room. And guess who they're all talking about at this moment, she thought wildly.

Then she realised that a girl was hurrying across the room to join them, a small dark girl with a set mouth and angry eyes. Now there was no mistaking the hostility in the atmosphere. What had she done? She wrenched her mind back to Laurie's diffident tones. 'I don't suppose you've ever heard of me? I used to give Ben a hand around the place——'

'Give him a hand!' the dark girl cried scathingly. Her gaze fixed on Christine smouldered with resentment. 'What he should be telling you is that he's been your uncle's head shepherd for the past eight years! He won't tell you, but I will! Ben thought the world of him. He often said that Laurie was like a son to him, that he couldn't have run Glendene without him——'

Laurie looked acutely embarrassed. 'Come off it, Jan. No need to——'

Taking not the slightest notice of the interruption, she swept on, 'She's going to hear the truth from someone else sooner or later, so why not now? It isn't *fair*!' the low tone throbbed with emotion. 'Now he hasn't even got a job, he hasn't anything—thanks to you. If only Ben——'

'What Jan's trying to say,' he broke in awkwardly, 'is that your uncle and I, we hit it off pretty well. We got on right from the beginning. Anyway, I'd better put you in the picture.

Old Ben was a member of the local Hunt and most of the guys here tonight are farmers living around the district who belong as well.' The band had started up once again and Christine had to strain her ears to catch the low

words. 'Over the years there've been no end of hunts over
our——' he broke off, a brick-red tide of colour suffusing
the blunt features. Hastily he amended the slip, 'At Glendene. Hunt teas, socials, dances, there've been lots of them
held here and this "do" tonight is a sort of send-off to the
old place. We figured the new owner—that is,' he said
flustered, 'you wouldn't want to be lumbered with an old
wreck like this. So we decided we'd have one last fling in
the old place, throw a few haybales around the walls, hire
a couple of the local boys to make music and give the place
a decent send-off——'

'You too,' the dark girl cut in, tight-lipped.

The colour had receded a little from Laurie's tanned
cheeks. Christine gathered that he was as anxious to avoid
the subject of his own affairs as his girl-friend was determined to draw attention to the matter of his having lost his
employment.

'Come along,' he was saying, 'you'd better come with me
and meet the folks.'

She shrank back nervously. 'No, it doesn't matter. I'll
meet them all ... some other time, I guess.' Suddenly she
was dreadfully weary, but she summoned a smile. 'It's
quite a drive down from Auckland to your neck of the
woods. I've left my hired Mini out in the yard.'

There was no mistaking the expression of relief that
crossed the boyish features. He said quickly, 'I'll take you
over to the house——'

'*Her* house, you mean,' said the dark girl with cruel
emphasis. 'It's not your home any longer and never will
be!'

For some reason Christine couldn't fathom the girl was
consumed with bitter anger—but it wasn't her fault, Christine thought. All at once the scene around her, the naked
light bulbs high above the smoke-filled room, the chatter
and laughter punctuated by the chink of glasses, blurred
out of focus. 'If you don't mind,' she murmured out of a
haze of weariness, 'I'd like to go to the house.'

'Sure, sure.' As Laurie turned away Jan laid a small

peremptory hand on his bare tanned arm. 'Don't go! Let someone else take her. Kevin! He won't mind.'

'Kevin?' Surprise tinged Laurie's tone. 'Why him?'

'Why not? He hasn't been dancing tonight. He never does when Andrea's away.' She raised her voice. 'Hi Kevin!'

Feeling as though she had become a piece of merchandise to be bandied from one stranger to another, Christine watched as Jan hurried towards a group of men who were gathered in the open doorway. A tall dark man who had been talking with the others turned to eye Jan enquiringly, then tossed his cigarette into the bushes. The next minute, walking with an easy grace, he strolled towards her. His eyes, of a smoky blue, swept her face. Cool distant eyes, no hint of friendliness there, no quick spark of masculine interest either, not this time. If she hadn't been so travel-weary Christine would have felt piqued at the novel sensation of being regarded by a new male acquaintance with complete indifference. It was almost—but of course that was ridiculous—as if the cold stare held a shade of contempt. Yet there was something about the dark compelling face that held her. An attractive voice too, rich and deep.

'What's the problem?'

'No problem.' It was Jan who answered. 'At least, not anything to worry about. Kevin, this is Christine Rowles, Ben's niece.' And to Christine, 'Kevin Hawke. Known around these parts as "The King",' she added laughingly.

'Nice to meet you, Miss Rowles.' Nice! He looked anything but pleased and clearly the sight of her gave him no joy. And why was he nicknamed 'the King', for heaven's sake? Close on the thought came another. Yet there was something about him, a sort of laconic strength as though that deceptively lazy voice concealed a sheathed vitality.

Christine wrenched her gaze away from the lean intelligent face and concentrated on Jan's voice. 'Laurie has a few things here to see to and Miss Rowles wants to go to the house. Could you help out?'

Once again Christine was aware of the cool blue stare,

but he inclined his head politely. 'How did you make your way here?'

'I've got a car outside. I hired one in Auckland when I got off the plane from London. Would you believe, I collected a puncture way down in the gorge on the way here. Luckily a Maori driver stopped his big transporter and came to my rescue.' She was nattering on wildly, but she couldn't seem to stop, even though she got an impression he hadn't the slightest interest in her movements. But there she was mistaken, for as they moved together towards the doorway he said coolly, 'Couldn't wait to get here, was that it?'

She ignored the irony in his tone. 'No, I couldn't'

As they stepped into the darkness outside she stumbled slightly, blinded by the sudden transition from the garish lights. He made no attempt to help her and she was determined she wouldn't do *that* again. She hurried along at his side, trying to match her steps to his long stride.

'I'll get your gear. Is this the car?' He moved towards the Mini.

'That's it.' She waited while he took her brand new suitcase from the back seat. Belatedly she realised it would have been more sensible of her to have let the folk here know the date of her arrival. As they moved towards the house she said slowly, 'I suppose Uncle Ben did have a housekeeper—or something?'

His voice was steel. 'He had a housekeeper.'

'Oh, that's a relief!' At least she thought something was going right in this crazy world into which she had stumbled.

'But she happens to be away for the night. Ella and Fred Montgomery were just about a part of the family here. Now they're away up country trying to find themselves a married-couple job on another farm.'

'Oh! But they mustn't do that!' Kevin Hawke had paused to open the gate and in the dimness she searched the closed face. 'Why couldn't they just stay on here the same as before, with me?'

He shrugged. 'That's up to you—here we are.'

Light streamed over the porch illuminating concrete paths surrounding a neatly kept brick house. Christine caught a glimpse of wide lawns sloping away from the dwelling, the pale blur of blossoming shrubs, then she realised he had hurried on ahead to switch on a light inside the house. He was standing waiting in the open doorway and because it seemed to her he was regarding her with barely-concealed impatience, she deliberately slowed her steps.

'Kitchen.' She had a brief impression of an immaculate room painted in green and white tonings, a long deep-freeze and cupboards taking up one wall, an electric range. Before she could fully take in her surroundings, however, Kevin Hawke was striding ahead, switching on another light to reveal a comfortably furnished lounge room where fluffy white sheepskin rugs were scattered over polished floors. She had barely time to take in the well-worn lounge suite with its floral covers and an old kauri table before he had led the way into a long passage with doors opening off from either side. 'Ella and Fred's room!' She caught a quick glimpse of a neatly covered double bed, a simple chest, a bookcase, then she was hurrying along beside him as still at breakneck speed he proceeded to open the door opposite. 'Guest room. *Your* room.' Did she imagine the ironic note in his voice? He dumped her suitcase on a low table and strode across the passage to fling open another door. 'Laurie's hang-out.'

In a sudden blaze of light there sprang to view an unmade bed on which lay a canvas holdall stuffed haphazardly with denim jeans and shirts. A guitar was tossed at the side of the bag.

Christine made no comment. She had scarcely time even had she been curious concerning the packed travel bag, for already her guide was flinging open a succession of doors near the end of the long passage. 'Bathroom, shower's next door, laundry.' She took a quick glance. It had to be quick if she weren't to miss seeing the rooms altogether.

She said in an attempt at lightness, 'Good old Uncle Ben. For a man who had always lived in the way-backs he must have been pretty up to date in his ideas.' For she had noticed in the laundry the automatic washing machine standing alongside a gleaming white electric dryer.

'Ella's idea,' her guide said shortly.

Christine sighed. What was the use? He just didn't approve of anything about her. Well, that suited her. Apparently he relished his enforced task of guiding her through the house about as much as she enjoyed having him show her around.

'That's about it!' Clearly he couldn't wait to get back with his friends in the crowded room next door.

As they moved back to the lounge room honesty impelled Christine to say, 'I hope it hasn't put anyone out my turning up here early. Like I said, I couldn't wait to get here.'

'So I gathered.' He paused in the doorway. 'Smoke?' He offered her a cigarette, but she shook her head.

'I mean——' Nervousness was making her run on. Nervousness? Or could it be the cool glance from the compelling dark face? She noticed now the deep lines running down on each side of his mouth, the firmly cut lips and chin. A strong face. The sort of man one could trust in other circumstances, of course, *any other circumstances*. 'I was so anxious to see my property.'

He struck a match, cupping a deeply bronzed hand around the flame. 'Actually it's not your property.'

Her brown eyes wide with alarm sought his face. 'What?'

'Not until next week,' came the laconic tones. 'I understand the settlement date when you're due to take over isn't until the last day of the month.'

'Yes,' she whispered, 'that's right.' How could she have overlooked such an all-important detail? She said on a breath, 'Stupid of me, I suppose, but I thought the house would be empty except for the housekeeper.'

He appeared to have lost interest in her problems. 'It

will be after tonight. Laurie's leaving right after the crowd
take off. He'll be staying at his girl-friend's place a few
miles up the road until he manages to jack up something
for himself.' A lift of strongly marked brows. 'You're not
nervous about staying here by yourself? Ella and Fred will
be back some time tomorrow, if only to collect their stuff
and to feed the dogs.'

Oh dear. Christine's heart fell. What a terrible upheaval
her arrival here had made to the lives of these people!
First Laurie, now Ella and Fred Montgomery. Perhaps when
she met the couple tomorrow she could arrange something,
persuade them to stay on at Glendene. She became aware
of his sardonic blue glance. 'You don't fancy it?'

'Staying here for the night, you mean? Oh, that doesn't
worry me.' She added airily, 'I'm a good sleeper.'

Again the ironic grin. 'That's what you think. Wait till
you hear the traffic rumbling past all through the early
hours. It churns up the hill, the big stuff.'

'Traffic?' She stared at him incredulously. 'But it's miles
from anywhere——'

'You reckon? It may look a quiet road, but it happens to
be on the direct route to the local saleyards. The big stock
trailers pass all through the night on their way to the
stockyards, trucks, trailers, transporters, the lot. It's just
bad luck that there's a sale on at the yards tomorrow.'

She regarded him suspiciously. 'You're having me on!'

'Why would I do that?' She was beginning to distrust the
bland expression in those smoky blue eyes. 'You'll see.'

He seemed, she thought crossly, to take a positive delight
in the prospect of her having a broken night's sleep. Aloud
she declared with spirit, 'Well, it won't worry me. I'm so
tired tonight I won't hear a thing!'

'Then, of course,' he murmured in deceptively mild accents, 'there's the stock to keep an eye on.'

'Stock?' At last he had succeeded in his attempts to
alarm her. 'What do you mean?'

'Nothing much.' He studied the glowing tip of his cigarette. 'Sheep, horses, pigs, dogs—they're always getting

loose and taking off down the highway.'

Thrusting aside her feelings of apprehension she made her voice light and casual. 'I don't mind.'

She could tell by the look in his eyes the direction in which his thoughts were drifting. A city girl, what would she know about handling stock? If it weren't that she was feeling so tired (or defeated?) she would let him know that she had been brought up in the English countryside and had had quite a lot of experience in the matter of caring for horses and dogs. Somehow, though, she suspected that nothing she could say would cut any ice with him. He appeared to have made up his mind to distrust her capabilities. Afraid of a pretty face? Now where had that thought sprung from?

She became aware of his glance that rested on her well-cut black pants-suit and as clearly as if he had spoken she tuned in on his thoughts. How could he know that the garments fashioned in the latest London style had been made on her sewing machine in the flat? Or that the expensive perfume she wore together with the luxuriously appointed travel gear had been gifts from her mother and stepfather on her departure for New Zealand?

She said on a sigh of relief, 'Oh well, if that's all I have to worry about——'

'Then there's the road outside the house.' Was he deliberately provoking her? Doing his utmost to get rid of her before she had even settled in?

She threw him a disbelieving look. 'That quiet country road——'

'Happens to be one of the main routes to the city. Traffic is fast and makes no allowance for wandering stock on the steep hill. What makes it even more dangerous,' he added as if for good measure, 'are the blind bends on either side of the rise. It's a killer in winter when the surface is icy.'

'I know, I saw the notice on my way up the hill. Isn't it lucky that it's summer time!'

'Summer's the worst time. The oil from the big transporters is slippery as hell, not to mention the greasy white line on the road that the motor-cyclists come to grief on.'

'My goodness,' she tried for flippancy, 'it's a miracle I ever arrived here today in one piece.' Forcing a smile (she seemed to have an endless supply of forced smiles tonight), she looked up into the closed dark face. 'You don't seem to think that I'll last very long here?'

'That's over to you, isn't it?' he said, and turned away. 'Night!' he flung the word over his shoulder.

She had a most un-Christine-like impulse to slam the door violently after him. Of all the self-opinionated, interfering, arrogant——

Good-looking, though, put in the small black goblin deep in her mind. Attractive too if you happen to go for that dark forceful type.

Well, I don't!

Famous last words, jeered the goblin in the split second before Christine banished him from her mind.

CHAPTER TWO

IN spite of her travel weariness Christine lay wakeful through the night. The events of the long day churned endlessly through her mind and always her thoughts reverted to Kevin Hawke. Maddening to have to admit that he had been right about the traffic grinding up the hill outside disturbing her rest.

For some reason she couldn't fathom he had taken a positive pleasure in her discomfiture and inexperience. Could it be a reactionary thing? Something connected with girls with blonde hair, dark eyes and an independent spirit? Oh, blast! She pummelled her pillow vigorously; she had more important matters on her mind at the moment, like adapting herself to new people and an entirely different life-style. It was no use; the dark mocking face continued to invade her thoughts.

At some time during the night she became aware of soft footfalls coming along the hall and she remembered Laurie and his half-packed travel bag. Presently she caught the sound of voices in the kitchen, a man and a girl's voice, and a little later she heard car engines revving up. Lights beamed through her window as vehicles moved down the drive.

As the hours went by she was aware of the grinding of heavy trucks as they took the long pull of the hill, driving through the night. Once again lights swept her windows as long stock trailers went by. It was a relief when daylight lightened the room and pulling aside the curtains, she let in bright sunshine. She would get up now and take a look around the place—*her* place. Somehow though, the bright joy of ownership had dimmed. She couldn't forget the hostility she had felt in the air on the previous night. But she would win them over, overcome that initial distrust of which she couldn't be unaware.

She took a quick warm shower, then got into well worn blue jeans and yellow body shirt and slipped her feet into rubber thongs. She ran a comb through her hair and the fine fair strands sprang back into natural waves.

There was something a little forbidding about the long silent passageway with its closed doors on either side but the kitchen when she reached it looked sunny and welcoming, the stainless steel surfaces of sink bench winking silver in the early morning light. A few minutes later she was out in the clearest air she had ever known, strolling around the neatly kept brick bungalow with its concreted path running around both sides of the dwelling. Spreading lawns were bordered with pink and white oleanders. From the front of the house a wide verandah looked out on fenced green paddocks and near at hand the road winding up and down the steep gradient of the hill.

Christine wandered around the side of the house towards the back door. How different everything looked in daylight! Ahead was the cleared slope of a hillside and beyond the hills, range upon range, faded into a blue haze of distance.

A narrow path led past orange and lemon trees towards a cluster of outbuildings and the mellow red timbers of a wool shed. Passing the sheepdogs chained in their kennels, she moved on towards double garages holding a tractor and a truck, a farm motorbike and a big serviceable car. She peered inside a shed where saddles and bridles hung on hooks on the wall, then took a winding path up a rise. Half way up the slope she paused at a fenced paddock where a small shaggy pony raised a curious head at her approach. Christine let herself in at the gateway and patted the thick coat. 'I'll be back to see you,' she promised, 'and with a carrot next time.'

She went on up the hill rising against the translucent blue of the sky. Further up the rise two mares grazed with their foals and opposite a big strapping grey of about seventeen hands cropped the lush green grass. As Christine paused at the fence he came trotting towards her. 'You're beautiful,' she caressed the soft muzzle. She stayed at the fence a long time, then wandered up the path once again. It wasn't until she reached the top of the rise that she caught sight of the sheep, clustered thickly on the opposite slopes. It seemed incredible, she couldn't take it in, that it all really did belong to her. All this plus a decrepit old hotel! Thinking of the hotel reminded her that she hadn't yet seen beyond the one large room. Not to worry, there was plenty of time to look around.

Once more back in the house she switched on the tall chrome hot water jug, mixed a mug of instant coffee and slipped a slice of bread into the toaster. She was rinsing the dishes in the sink when the flow of water in the tap dribbled to a stop. Now what? She had noticed a big concrete tank in the yard. Surely it hadn't run dry? Frantically she turned the tap, to no effect. Was she to spend the day without water? she thought in panic.

'Hello!' She jumped in surprise and turned to face a

plump red-headed boy of perhaps seven years who had come to stand at her side. 'I'm Patrick. Are you the new boss?'

'Yes—look, do you know anything about the taps here? There doesn't seem to be any water.'

Patrick stood on the tips of his bare feet and peered into the sink. 'You have to turn on the pump.'

'Pump?' Christine felt unutterably relieved to have the answer to her problem. 'Where is it?'

'Outside. Come on, I'll show you.'

Her companion vanished and Christine hurried after him. He led the way towards the concrete tank and bent to flick the switch of an electric motor. Immediately a loud noise filled the air.

'When do I turn it off?' Christine shouted above the din.

'In half an hour!' he screamed. He regarded her curiously. 'Don't you know *anything*?—Hey! My pony Trixie! She's got out of the paddock!' It was true. Christine's horrified gaze went to the wide driveway where the small white pony she had seen this morning was trotting unconcernedly across the busy road. The next moment there was a squeal of brakes at the top of the hill. Quick as a flash Patrick had hurried away and Christine followed the boy down the driveway. As she reached the open gate she was aware of a red car pulled up ahead of a long line of vehicles that were banked up on the highway—a silver milk tanker, a car trailing a horse float, a truck.

'I've got him!' Luckily the pony had a halter around his neck, and luckily too, Christine thought, there was no traffic advancing in the opposite direction as Patrick guided the pony back through the opening.

She went with the boy while he returned the pony to his paddock. 'I wonder how the gate got open,' Patrick said curiously. Christine was wondering too. She had an uneasy suspicion that in her excitement she might just have not fastened the catch securely. And what of the big timber gate leading on to the busy highway? It stood wide open providing a ready-made escape route for any wandering stock. It was too late, for even as she turned she caught sight of a large pig that was moving down the driveway. At once Christine took off in pursuit, flinging over her shoulder to Patrick as she ran, 'You see to the gate and I'll go after the pig!'

Fortunately, she realised a few minutes later, the animal had paused just clear of the opening and she thought she might still be in time to close the heavy gate and prevent the escape. That was what she thought. For the gate, clearly in need of repair, was heavier than she would have imagined and stuck firmly on a tree-trunk embedded in the earth beneath. All her efforts to shift it were to no avail and Patrick's help made not the slightest difference. 'How come,' he panted red-faced with his efforts, 'that you're bigger than me and you can't shift it?'

'It's not a matter of size,' Christine said crossly. She made a last desperate effort and the timbered gate fell flat on the ground. To her dismay no amount of struggling on her part could raise it.

'Laurie can lift it easy!' puffed Patrick. 'He'll be mad if the pig gets out. It's his pig.'

'*He'll* be mad!' Christine's face was scarlet with frustration and exertion. 'It's all his fault! He should have fixed the gate instead of leaving it like this.'

'He said he would, only it wasn't his any more and he didn't care anyway!'

'He can darn well fix it when he comes back!' All at once she realised that the responsibility for farm repairs no longer lay with her uncle's employee. '*Someone* will have to mend it!'

Patrick appeared to have other matters on his mind. 'He'll be mad about Daisy too.' With the morbid satisfaction of one imparting bad news he added, 'She's his best sheepdog, and now she's slipped her chain and gone. I know because I went to look at her this morning when I went to feed Trixie and she wasn't there.'

'I don't care where she is.' Christine could have wept

with mortification. She had been so confident she could be
left in charge of her own property, and look what had
happened! In the matter of a few short hours every animal
that could make an escape had given it a go. She gave a
last vicious wrench at the gate which remained as im-
movable as ever and straightened, flushed and hot and
angry, to meet the amused gaze of—wouldn't you know
it—Kevin Hawke. Seen in the clear light of day he appeared even more devastatingly attractive than she remembered. She had never been more glad to see anyone—
only because he was a man, of course. Right at this
moment she would have welcomed the sight of any male so
long as he possessed a pair of strong arms.

'Let me.' A swift effortless movement and the gate was
once again firmly in place.

'Thank you,' Christine said on a sigh of relief. 'I'll never
open it again. I'll climb over it, do anything...' Flustered,
she realised her dishevelled appearance. She must look a
whole lot different from the girl he had surveyed with such
indolent indifference last night. But it didn't matter. Seeing
he hadn't noticed her appearance last night he wouldn't be
likely to feel any more interested in her now. She heard
herself saying crossly, 'Why on earth didn't someone here
have the gate fixed? You'd think with such a busy road—'

'You'll have to ask Laurie about that, won't you?' The
cool tones brought her to her senses.

Uttering a wild whoop the small boy ran off, guiding the
pig back to his pen somewhere at the back of the house.
For something to say Christine murmured, 'How did you
know——'

Kevin shrugged broad shoulders beneath a crisp open-
necked cotton shirt. 'Just a calculated guess. Some of the
guys were fairly merry when they left the party last night.
It was on the cards that someone could have left the gate
open.'

Her brown eyes opened wide and she felt a flicker of
remorse. Although she could scarcely believe such a thing

possible it seemed she had misjudged him. 'And you came back here this morning specially——'

The sardonic curl of the firmly moulded lips should have warned her. 'Not especially. I just happened to be passing. I was on my way into town to meet someone and saw that you were in trouble wrestling with the gate. It's not the sort of thing you can miss.'

'No,' she said deflated, 'I don't suppose it is.'

For a man with an appointment in town he appeared to have all the time in the world. Thumbs tucked in the pockets of hip-hugging jeans, he was saying, 'So you've met up with Patrick?'

'But I don't know where he comes from. One of the nearby farms, I suppose?'

'That's right. He belongs to the Smiths. They live right opposite and are your nearest neighbours. Patrick keeps his pony over here at the moment——'

She looked up, animated and excited. 'I know, the little white shaggy one. I saw him this morning. He's a pet.'

'That's Trixie, Ben offered to get him ready for Patrick to ride. Handle the pony, give him some exercise, get him used to the saddle. He just about had him trained when he bought it. Oh well, that's the way it goes. Laurie took over from there, but the pony's just about ready for Patrick to take home now. The kid spends a lot of time over here with Bill and Laurie. Could be,' once again she caught the quizzical glance, 'he might be quite a help to you in some ways.'

'He's a nice little fellow.' She looked after Patrick who was approaching them down the long drive. 'He's been a big help to me already. Honestly, I don't know how I would have got on without him, with the electric pump and everything. Only trouble was,' she murmured wryly, 'that telling me how to do things seemed to go to his head. He kept on saying to me, "How come you're so big and I'm so little and you don't know *anything*!"'

Kevin laughed heartily. He would, when the joke was against her. In spite of herself Christine couldn't help laughing a little herself, her complaint sounded so ridiculous when she put it into words.

' 'Bye!' They watched the boy as carefully he negotiated the two lines of traffic on the road and opened a gate opposite.

'You'll be selling up here, of course?' The laconic tones took her by surprise and she regarded him with indignant brown eyes. 'Sell Glendene? I wouldn't dream of such a thing! I'm sure,' she protested, 'that Uncle Ben would have wanted me to keep it.'

His gaze hardened and she broke off. What had she said now, for goodness' sake, to bring the steely look back to the blue eyes?

'Are you?'

She was aware that he was regarding her closely. For a man who appeared to regard her with distrust and almost hostility, he was showing an awful lot of interest in her affairs.

'I shouldn't imagine,' his cool glance swept her face, 'that Te Weka would hold much appeal for a girl like you.'

So he had noticed her appearance. Oh, he'd noticed all right and disapproved. Well, she couldn't help her looks. Her voice was tight. 'What do you mean?'

'Isolated position, no discos, no restaurants—not at any rate to be compared with the sort of thing you would have been used to. Nothing to do, nowhere to go.' His eyes said, 'Your clothes, your whole appearance sets you in a world apart from life out here.' What was he saying now? 'Scarcely your scene, I would think, a farm on an island lying to the deep south of the Pacific Ocean over a thousand miles from anywhere.'

'I just might like it. If you're going by what happened this morning——'

He brushed that aside. 'Happens all the time in the country. Stock wanders out on to the road or a drover's steers wander in. A country girl would take it all in her stride, but a Londoner like you——'

She said fiercely, 'I wasn't always a Londoner. For your

information, I was brought up in the country. I spent half my life on a farm.'

'I can imagine. Nice orderly little farmlet down in Devon——'

'Yes, but ...' It was no use. Apparently Kevin had made up his mind about her inefficiency, her general inability to cope with local conditions and that was that.

'There's one part of the property you couldn't sell or even give away. You might as well put a match to the heap of old timber, that's what your uncle planned to do with it.'

'You mean the old hotel?'

'What else? You saw what it was like last night. It's a ruin, and what it would cost to bring it back to some sort of order is nobody's business.'

'It didn't look all that bad last night,' she faltered, 'but I haven't really seen it yet.'

'Prepare for a shock, then,' he told her in his laconic way and as if by common consent they strolled towards the building. She had to admit that on closer viewing it did look rather dreadful. The sagging verandah timbers looked scarcely safe to venture on and the front door swung on its hinges with a melancholy grating sound. They went around to the rear of the building and he flung open a door. As Christine peered into the dim and dusty interior she realised that the premises had been used as a haybarn.

'Want to see any more?' Like Patrick, Kevin seemed to take a sadistic delight in passing on bad news. 'I wouldn't advise you to set foot upstairs, not unless you believe in living dangerously and have a fully paid up life insurance policy. The top storey is definitely on the way out.'

She shook her head. 'The big main room,' she persisted forlornly, 'it didn't look so tumbledown last night.'

'Think so?'

Together they moved along a dim passage and as they went from room to room Christine's spirits dropped still further. An old disused kitchen that had evidently remained untenanted for many years. A neglected bathroom with a stained bath and cracked wall mirror. Even the big lounge

room that on the previous evening had appeared fairly
presentable had clearly been given a façade for one night
only.

'I see what you mean,' Christine said slowly. The garish
lights in naked bulbs left burning since last night illuminated cobwebs that festooned the windows. Torn pink paper
streamers hanging limply from dust-coated beams overhead served only to emphasise the depressing state of dis-
repair and decay. 'The stale cigarette smoke doesn't help,'
she tried to sound cheerful, 'and nor do all these empty
glasses.'

'You're right there. Come on, let's get rid of them!'
Surprisingly he was actually offering to help her, but now
she was too numbed to care. He found an empty cardboard
carton and stacked away empty beer and champagne glasses while she piled tumblers and ashtrays in a box and
carried them over to the house.

In the kitchen she ran hot water in the sink, squirted in
detergent and attacked the pile of glassware. I'm not
beaten yet, she told herself, and vigorously rubbed at a glass
ashtray.

Kevin followed her. He picked up a tea-towel and polished a crystal champagne goblet with care. Housetrained
by his wife? she wondered. Funny to think that she hadn't
imagined him as a married man. He didn't have a married
look somehow—arrogant, self-sufficient, interfering in
other folk's affairs. Yet there he was drying a mounting pile
of glassware and crystal goblets. There were an awful lot of
glasses and the thought came to her that though she hated
to admit it, his help provided a bright note on a singularly
depressing day.

'Have you any plans as to how you're going to manage?'
Kevin seemed to be a man who was determined to get
down to the nitty-gritty. Could that be the reason he was
helping her with the drying of the glassware? So that he
could quiz her about her affairs? 'If you're not planning to
sell up the place then what——'

The solution came to her in a flash. 'I'll just have to

employ a manager, someone who's experienced in sheep farming. There must be plenty of men around the district who'd fulfil the requirements— I know!' her face brightened. 'I'll ask Laurie to stay on here and manage the place. I don't know why I didn't think of him before. He's used to the work, he knows the place and everything. It's the perfect solution!'

Once again she saw Kevin's expression harden. 'It won't work. If you're thinking of asking Laurie to carry on here you can save yourself the trouble. He won't consider it for a moment.'

'Why not?' She was warming to the idea with every passing minute. 'He's looking for a position. He could stay on here at the house just as he did before.'

'He won't, you know.' He sounded so definite on the subject that perversely Christine felt she had to dispute his opinion. Kevin Hawke didn't know everything about everyone, even though he appeared to believe he did.

'I don't see why not!' she challenged him, and looked him full in the face. Only for a moment. For a quiver ran along her nerves and hurriedly she dropped her gaze. What was this? What was happening between herself and this stranger? A force, unseen but potent, flashed between them. What if he too were aware of it? Apparently not, she thought in relief the next moment as the deep quiet tones broke the spell. 'I'll tell you why not! You'll be hearing the story from someone else before long. You may as well have it straight!'

Christine held her breath and washed the same glass for the third time.

'Laurie was your uncle's right-hand man. He kept the show on the road. For the past few years the old man's health wasn't the best and he came to depend on Laurie for the real work around the place. Ben didn't do much more than supervise around the farm. Oh, he bred a few horses, rode around the boundaries now and again, but it was Laurie who did all the main work, saw to the horse-breaking, the mustering, the shearing. Over the years Laurie had a heck of a lot of offers of jobs with higher pay. Everyone for miles around knew him for a terrific worker, but he stuck with your uncle through the good years and the lean ones. He was just a lad when Ben took him on as a shepherd. That was eight years ago and he never worked for anyone else.'

She regarded him attentively. 'It's a wonder then that Uncle Ben didn't leave Glendene to him. He certainly deserved it.'

Kevin said dryly, 'That was the general idea. Ben never made any secret of the fact. It was an understood thing that the place would belong to Laurie some day, although he's such a conscientious guy he would have worked hard anyway. He's built that way, straightforward as they come and wrapped in the farming scene. You didn't ever meet Ben?'

Christine shook her head. 'I scarcely knew of his existence. He was just my father's brother who'd gone out to New Zealand years and years ago and had lost touch with the family.'

'That's what I thought.' Something in the tone of his voice troubled her. 'You never got the story of how your uncle died, I suppose?'

'No.' A shadow passed over her face. 'Just what the lawyer here told me when I rang through from London. That it was sudden, a heart attack, all over in a minute.' She glanced towards him in some alarm. 'It was like that, wasn't it?'

'That's how it happened. They found his car slewed off the road. He was slumped over the wheel with an unsigned will in his coat pocket. According to what he told Fred that morning Ben had got to thinking about his health problem and had at last got around to making a new will leaving everything he owned to Laurie. He planned to sign the document in the lawyer's office in town, had an appointment that day with his lawyer at three o'clock. He was on his way there when they found him dead in his car, at two.'

Christine had turned very pale. 'I didn't know,' she whispered. 'Thanks for telling me.'

He said shortly, 'If I hadn't someone else would. It's no secret around Te Weka that Ben always intended Laurie to have the place when he checked out. It was good thinking on Ben's part, would have worked out too if only he'd signed that paper in the lawyer's office the week before. But old Ben was always one for going into things thoroughly, he wanted to take his time and read every word of that paper. It was bad news for Laurie that Ben collected a fatal heart attack before he got to town and the old will that he'd signed twenty years earlier still stood.'

'And I was the only blood relation.' At last she was getting the better of the sense of shock, trying to pull her thoughts together. 'I still don't see why Laurie couldn't stay on here the same as ever. He wouldn't lose by it.' The hard mocking light in Kevin's eyes made her voice tremble a little. 'Financially, I mean.'

'Don't you, Miss Rowles? Well, let me tell you something. You can forget about putting that proposition of yours to Laurie. You haven't a hope in hell in that direction. Laurie's one man you'll never manage to twist around your finger. He might look young and unsophisticated, he is too, but he's a Scot and once he's made up his mind that's it!'

Stung, she said with spirit, 'You seem to know him very well.'

'I do. Laurie was brought up by my mum and dad. He was left on his own as a kid and my parents took him into their home. I feel sort of responsible,' he drawled.

'A father figure?' she couldn't resist the jibe.

Kevin merely regarded her with his enigmatic glance. 'Something like that.' After a moment he added, 'What I'm getting at is that you'll be saving yourself a lot of disappointment if you don't put that idea of yours to Laurie. It won't do you any good, you know.' He was positively gloating, she thought angrily. 'Take it from me, this is one man you won't be able to do what you like with, even with your looks! You're very pretty, Miss Rowles, you don't need me to tell you that, but this is one time when you won't succeed in getting your own way.'

A strange little thrill shot through her. She didn't know whether to be pleased or angry. Despite his offhanded manner, his cool assessing glance, he had noticed her. If he were insinuating that conscious of the power of beauty she was accustomed to using her attractions to attain her own ends, if he were taking it for granted that she was spoiled and selfish ...

'You could be wrong about that!' Her quick indignant glance flashed to his face and once again she was forced to drop her gaze. There was something disturbing in those dark blue eyes, a smouldering flicker that did things to her composure and made her long to get the better of him one way or another. 'Like to bet?'

Again the infuriating drawl. 'I never bet on certainties. Right!' he tossed the tea-towel down on the bench, 'I'd better get cracking!'

'Oh yes, you had to meet someone in town.'

He grinned, 'She'll keep.'

Confused, she said, 'Well, thanks for helping with the glasses, Mr King.'

A half-mocking smile touched his lips. 'Hawke's the name. See you!' He was gone, hurrying down the path with his long easy stride, whistling a tune. No doubt she mused he was feeling quite triumphant at the moment, having taken the trouble to acquaint her with the true position here. Only at that moment did Jan's words come back to her mind. 'They call him "the King".' It served him right if she had forgotten his name, flustering her the way he had. Viciously she twisted the dishcloth and wished she could wring *his* neck!

CHAPTER THREE

FLUSHED, humiliated, indignant, Christine was so involved with thoughts of Kevin Hawke that it was a while before the full significance of his disclosure struck her. She stood motionless, staring with unseeing eyes over the empty hills. The parts of the puzzle were falling into place with devastating clarity—the atmosphere of barely concealed hostility of which she had been conscious since the moment she stepped into the old building, Laurie's reluctance to have anything to do with his supplanter. Look at the way in which he had delegated the matter of seeing her to the house last night to someone else. Because it was a situation too painful for him to face? If only she had known all this beforehand she would never have made the journey.

Could it be that the story Kevin Hawke had told her wasn't the truth? She had only his word for it, the word of a stranger. Yet somehow in spite of his ruthless disregard for her feelings she trusted him. All right then, say it was true, what then? Restlessly she wandered through the house without taking in her surroundings. No longer was there any feeling of excitement in exploring house or grounds; Kevin Hawke had very effectively seen to that. For whichever way you looked at the problem it led back to the painful conclusion that Glendene wasn't hers, not really. She had gained the property only through a quirk of fate while the man who had worked for years to bring the sheep farm into production had nothing to show for his labours. It was a moral thing and whether she wanted to or not she was forced to the inevitable conclusion that she wasn't entitled to Glendene, not really. When Laurie came back to the house to collect his stock she would tell him so. It was as simple as that, were she to continue to live with her conscience.

Restlessly she went out of the back door and wandered up the green slope to the paddock where the grey thoroughbred grazed. He nickered softly as she paused at the fence, a carrot extended in her hand. She wondered about the rough jumps erected on the ground. Perhaps her uncle had put them up with the intention of teaching Patrick to take his pony over the painted rails. She would have thought nothing of taking the low barricades on her mare Misty before the accident. Maybe if she practised on these jumps she could get back her confidence and take her mount over the high barbed wire fences she glimpsed on the slopes rising around her. Why not now, on the grey horse right here to hand? Even as she turned away to get saddle and bridle from the harness shed she knew she couldn't make the attempt. She was still a prisoner of her nerves. She told herself that she hadn't the right to saddle the grey hunter, that he didn't belong to her—not until next week, as that horrible Kevin Hawke had taken the trouble to point out to her. Deep down, however, she knew that wasn't the real reason why she had changed her mind. It was back again, the cold fear, the trembling over which she had no control.

The endless day dragged on. The telephone was silent and Patrick failed to make an appearance. Late in the afternoon Christine wandered out to the verandah, idly watching a mass of black cattle flowing over the roadway and up on the grassy bank opposite. All at once she realised that a car that had been weaving a slow passageway among the straggling steers at the roadside was turning in at the gate. The housekeeper and her husband! Hurriedly Christine went to the kitchen. She switched on the tall chrome electric jug and threw a cloth over the table. She was arranging biscuits on a plate when a feminine voice reached her from the pathway outside the window. 'Look, Fred, the windows are open. Laurie must have beaten us back.'

Almost Christine could have burst into laughter at the expression of astonishment on the two faces as the couple

opened the door to the sight of a strange girl in their
kitchen. She had a swift impression of a big rawboned man
with sparse greying hair and a kindly expression, of a
neatly dressed little woman, sparrow-thin, with cropped
dark hair and shrewd hazel eyes.

'Hello,' Christine greeted them cheerfully. 'You must be
Ella and Fred. I'm Christine. You know? Christine Rowles.'

The smile on the woman's tanned face froze into a
glance of disapproval. 'Oh, *that* Christine!'

'Now, now, Mum——' The husband, it seemed to Christine, was more kindly disposed towards her (a typical male
reaction)? Or maybe he was more adroit at hiding his feelings. A work-roughened hand shot towards her. 'Glad to
meet you, Miss Rowles! We've been expecting you,' he
went on in his slow deliberate tones, 'isn't that right, Mum?'

'Mum' avoided Christine's glance. She said tightly, 'We
thought you wouldn't be arriving here until next week, the
takeover day.'

'I'm sorry I didn't let you know. Honestly, I wasn't sure
if anyone was in the house or not. Besides,' Christine
smiled winningly, 'I was in such a hurry to get here, I just
couldn't wait.'

The woman's face tensed and to forestall the bitter words
she sensed were coming Christine said quickly, 'I've made
coffee. I expect you'll feel like a drink. Have you—come
far?'

It was Fred who answered. He was tugging at his tie,
throwing it on the table, and she guessed that he was un-
accustomed to such restrictions. 'Too far, and all for
nothing as it turned out. It's not that we can't find a job,
mind you. Married couples in the country are pretty
sought after, especially folk like Ella and me with lots of
experience. But we don't want to take anything when we
leave here—excuse me, I'll just go and wash my hands.'

When he returned to the room Christine had poured
coffee into pottery beakers. Everyone sat down at the table
where the late afternoon sunshine streamed in at the open
window.

Fred stirred his coffee reflectively. 'I don't mind telling you it's been a shock to all of us, old Ben going out like a light without a moment's warning!'

'He was in the car when it happened?' Christine prompted.

'That's right. On the road to town buzzing along in his old bus as happy as you please, then crash! the car runs off the road and the next motorist to come along finds him slumped over the wheel with the engine still running. It was too bad for all of us,' he said on a sigh, 'that it had to happen that day of all days.'

Christine sat very still. 'Why that day especially?'

'Why, because ... because ...' The honest face reddened beneath the tan as he caught his wife's warning glance. But Christine had heard enough, more than enough. So it was true, every word that interfering Kevin Hawke had told her.

'Ben had a special appointment in town that day,' Ella put in guardedly. 'Something that was important to him.' She added in a low emotional tone, 'And to the rest of us as well.'

'You've had a look around outside?' Christine guessed that Fred was trying to change the conversation.

'Oh yes, I came here yesterday you see. Everything seems to be kept in such good order, and the gardens are really lovely, all those flowering shrubs.'

Fred nodded. A shadow passed over his features. 'Mum and I planted all those oleanders, took years to get them to the size they are now. They're—they *were*,' carefully he corrected himself, 'a sort of hobby with us. That's right, eh, Mum?'

'They were,' Ella echoed in a low tone. She lifted eyes washed clear of all hope to Christine's gaze. 'It's all yours now. That old will that Ben made years and years ago ... you're his only relative, it seems.'

'That's true.' Christine leaned forward appealingly. 'But there's no need for either of you to leave here. I'd be so glad if you would stay. I'll need all the help I can have, you know.'

Two pairs of eyes regarded her incredulously. 'You're not planning to stay, *a girl like you?*'

Christine was fast coming to hate that phrase. What sort of girl did they take her for, for heaven's sake? A fashion model, an empty-headed nit?

Fred was saying slowly, awkwardly. 'It's a bit of a shock to Mum and me. You see, we thought you'd be sure to sell up right away. We never dreamed that you'd want to keep the place going.'

'We thought,' his wife put in in her quick way, 'that you'd come out to Glendene, take one look at the place, then put it on the market right away.'

Christine smiled again. 'It just goes to show how little you know me! No, I'll be staying for a while anyway, I haven't decided yet for how long. If you would stay too under the same terms as before with everything going along just the same as when Uncle Ben was here——'

She caught the sudden brightening of both faces. 'Will we?' Fred looked immensely relieved.

'What he means,' cut in Ella in her quick nervous tones, 'is that we'll think about it. There are a lot of things to consider, but we'll let you know when we've had a chance to talk it over.'

'Of course. I only hope the answer is "yes".' They're suspicious of me and angry and hurt because of Uncle Ben's will, she thought. But I'll make them like me. They can't go on hating me, all of them, because of something I knew nothing about, they just can't!

She was out in the grounds gathering big yellow daisies from the flower border for the vases when Fred came to join her.

'Just wanted you to know, miss, that if it's up to me there's no question about taking up that offer of yours. It's just what I would like, and no doubt about it.'

She snipped a spray of yellow spikes. 'Is Ella happy about the arrangement too, do you think?'

He hesitated for a moment. 'Of course she is, but she won't admit it, not right away. She'll hold out for a while so as not to seem too eager, but she'll come around, you'll see.'

'That's super. There'll be so much that both of you could tell me about, and I'll need all the help I can get.'

'Only too pleased, miss——'

'Christine,' she corrected with a smile.

'Christine, then. Pity you don't ride.' He seemed to be speaking his thoughts aloud. 'Ben's horse Trooper needs exercising. He's safe as a house, but he needs an experienced rider, got a mouth of iron. He's so strong he's difficult to manage once he gets out of a walk. He's going to miss not joining in the hunt meetings this season, is Trooper.'

Christine made no comment beyond a non-committal, 'I guess.'

'Look,' Fred appeared to be struggling with something on his mind, 'there's a little matter I'd like to talk over with you if you don't mind my shoving my oar in. It's important like or I wouldn't mention it.'

'What is it?' To save him embarrassment she went on snipping daisies.

'You'll be needing someone to manage the place? An experienced bloke who's used to sheep farming?'

'I know, I know.' She decided to sound him out. 'I was wondering about Laurie, do you think that he——'

'Sorry, miss—Christine, I mean—but there's not a chance of his staying on. He's made up his mind to look for a manager's job somewhere else. They're thinking of getting married next year, he and Jan. They'll have to wait a while, though, save a bit longer if they're ever to get that farm of their own now that——' He broke off and after a moment mumbled, 'I mean, with prices going up and all that.'

Christine, however, was well aware of what he had been about to say. There was no need for anyone to spell it out to her, not now.

'I could look out for a manager for you if you want me to,' Fred was saying. 'Not that anyone could touch Laurie. He just about worked himself to death on the place, but you'll need to have a man who's reliable, and I know most of the station staff around the district.'

'Thanks, Fred, I'd appreciate it if you would.'

He said awkwardly, 'If you don't mind my saying so I wouldn't offer the job to Laurie. He's a bit touchy about the whole thing right at the moment—here he comes now.' A truck towing a horse float was moving up the path from the gate.

A few minutes later Laurie came strolling towards them. 'Hi, Fred!' His glance rested for a moment on Christine's face, then with a barely perceptible nod he moved on in the direction of the stables. She thought: He can't bear the sight of me here, and no wonder. An interloper in the place he's come to regard as his own home. She watched as he emerged from the stables and began to climb a green slope, a saddle, bridle and sheepskin over his arm.

'He's off to saddle up one of the stock ponies and take a ride around some of the boundary fences,' Fred told her.

'Will he be away long?'

'That depends on whether he comes on a gap in the wires and has to put sheep back into their paddock. Or it could be the steers that have broken through.'

Christine waited a long time for Laurie to return and at last, feeling restless and unhappy, she went to her room. If she intended to remain here for a period, and somehow in spite of the shattering disclosure of yesterday she still didn't want to go, she might as well start unpacking her suitcase. Somehow, though there was no joy in hanging the crisp new tops and shorts and slacks in the big old wardrobe.

It wasn't until dinner time that Laurie appeared once again. Freshly shaven and wearing a cool cotton shirt and

Crimplene shorts, he took his place next to Christine at the table.

'Hello!' She put all her charm into her brightest smile, but she might just as well not have troubled herself for all the response her greeting evoked.

'Hi.' His brooding glance slid away from her face. Then with an effort at cheerfulness he glanced towards Fred. 'What's been happening around here since I left, anything?'

What's been happening? I could tell you a thing or two, Christine thought, but you wouldn't want to hear about it, not from me!

'You'll have to ask Christine about that,' Fred was saying in his slow deliberate tones.

At least, she thought wryly, she had one friend at Glendene.

Laurie ignored the suggestion. 'With you, I mean?'

'Nothing much to report. The phone's been as dead as a doornail since Ella and I got back a while ago.'

Laurie didn't appear to be listening. Suddenly his gaze swept meaningfully towards the older man. 'You know what I'm getting at. Have you had any luck with your enquiries around the place?' Christine knew he was referring to the job-hunting activities of the couple.

Fred said hesitatingly, a grin tugging at his lips, 'We've had one offer that's worth considering——'

Ella, pouring tea, put in in her quick sharp tone, 'We'll tell you all about it later.'

The two men and Ella went on to discuss matters concerned with stock and farm work. Christine sat forgotten, picking at the delectable chicken salad Ella had prepared and wishing the meal was over. Laurie couldn't have made it more plain that she was unwelcome and unwanted.

'How about you, Laurie?' She brought her mind back to Ella's curious tones. 'What did you think of the places you went to see?'

'Not much.' Defeat and despondency coloured the heavy tones. He said on a sigh, 'Oh well, I don't have to do anything in a hurry.' He gave a laugh that seemed to crack in the middle. 'After all, I'm still on the job here—until Monday.'

Christine thought she had never seen such misery in a man's eyes.

He loves this place, she thought, it's really a part of him. No wonder, when he's worked so hard at getting it to what it is today. In that moment she knew what she must do. She had known all along really, only she had been dodging the issue, trying, hoping to find some alternative. She would *make* him listen to her.

After she had helped Ella with the dinner dishes she went in search of Laurie. She looked in the stables, the workshop, the garages, then she climbed the grassy rise. A haze of twilight hung over the surrounding hills, painting purple shadows in the gullies. Half way up the slope Uncle Ben's grey hunter was a dark silhouette against the pale primrose afterglow of the setting sun. Just at first she didn't see the man standing at the fence.

Christine hurried up the hill. This time he wouldn't be able to avoid her.

As she neared him he tossed away his cigarette, grinding it into the grass with the heel of his boot.

She came to the fence to stand at his side. 'That's Trooper, isn't it? We got acquainted yesterday.'

'That's right.' She caught a half-apologetic note in the low tones. 'I didn't think you'd be interested in your uncle's hunter or I would have taken you around the place. The stock ponies are further up the hill.'

Christine came to his rescue. 'There hasn't been much time, has there? Anyway, I had a good look around on my own—well, not quite on my own. Patrick came over to see to his pony. He often comes over here to look after Trixie, he told me.'

'Sure does. The kid just about lived here when Ben was around.' Laurie sounded abstracted. 'You like horses, then? Ever done any riding or hunting? Your uncle was a keen hunting man.'

'Oh yes!' Just in time she avoided the trap. 'Riding, I

mean. That is,' now she was the one to suffer embarrassment, 'I know which side of a horse you get on and the way you hop off.'

'You haven't been tossed off yet?'

'Have I ever! Oh yes, I know all about that part of it too—did Ella or Fred tell you that I'm staying on here?'

He kicked a restless foot against a fence post and she caught his low mutter. 'They did say something about it.'

She decided to come right out with what she had to say. 'I've asked them both if they'll keep on living here just the same as when Uncle Ben was here. They're thinking it over, but I'm hoping they will. I just wanted to tell you, Laurie——'

'If you're thinking of offering me the manager's job,' his voice was tight, 'you can save your breath! If you're looking for someone to run the outfit for you you'll have to look around for some other guy. Sorry, Miss Rowles, but that's the way it is.'

She said with a smile, 'Know something? I won't be needing anyone else for the job.'

'How d'you mean?' Bewilderment tinged the low tone.

'Just that I'm not taking on Glendene. I'm transferring it to you! We'll go in to the lawyer in town tomorrow and fix it all up with him. Don't look so staggered! I really won't miss it. I never really owned it. The date I was supposed to take over the place is Monday, remember? I've been thinking things over ever since I discovered what's been happening here. I mean, about Uncle Ben intending you to have Glendene all the time and then meeting with the accident on his way to sign the papers——'

He cut in tersely, 'Who told you about that?'

'A man who stopped his car on the road and came to my rescue yesterday. That was when the pony and the pig seemed determined to commit suicide on the main highway. You've no idea how pleased I was to have someone fix the gate for me. I could tell by the way Ella and Fred were talking that what he'd told me was true.'

'It's true enough, but if you think I'd let you hand over

the place to me just like that——' He braced himself. 'I couldn't possibly accept it.'

'I don't know,' said Christine laughingly, 'how you're going to stop me!' Before he could protest further she swept on, 'I'd better warn you there's a catch to the proposition. Let's keep all this strictly between ourselves. I mean, no one need know about it, not even Jan. I feel badly enough as it is about coming here, messing up people's lives, without all the upheaval of another changeover. No one need know except the lawyer, at least not until the whole thing is legally settled. What do you say?'

'Well ...' Disbelief and an incredulous happiness mingled in his glance.

'Everything will go along just the same as before except that on the face of it I'll be the owner, for a little while. You see, I've learned a few things this weekend. I had no idea that it was you who'd made Glendene the prosperous place it is, that Uncle Ben had just pottered around——'

'That wasn't his fault,' Laurie cried defensively, 'he used to be a terrific worker. It was only in the last few years when his health gave out that he stopped doing much around the place, but he was always there with advice. He'd had years of experience and he had a good business head. Glendene was his whole life.'

'And yours?' she said gently.

'I—guess so.'

Christine pressed her advantage over the man who clearly was stunned by the unexpected turn of events. 'Fred let out that you and Jan were planning to be married next year. With the property and house you would have a good start.'

'That was the idea.'

'Why not? It can still happen. All you need to do is to put up with me around the place for a few months, then I'll be off and away, and when I've gone back to England you can make it known that you were the owner and not my manager or head shepherd, whatever, all the time.'

'If you really mean it.' The low tones were hoarse with

emotion. All at once Laurie wasn't shy or diffident any longer. 'You can't realise what you're saying! You're throwing away the inheritance of a lifetime. There's big money involved. You can't toss it away just like that, as if it were nothing.'

'Don't worry, I've seen all the accounts and the lawyer made the value of Glendene pretty clear to me when I was in London. But it isn't mine to give, it's yours—Oh, not legally, I know,' as he made to remonstrate, 'but that's what Uncle Ben really wanted, that's the way it has to be. You know I'm right.'

'What can I say?' His voice throbbed with excitement. 'Having Glendene for my own is something I've been counting on for years, but to take it from you——'

'You'll be doing me a favour! If you only knew the bad time I've been having with my conscience lately. I can't face any more sleepless nights. Truly, I wouldn't dream of keeping an inheritance that I'd only gained through a trick of fate.'

He said incredulously, 'You really do mean it.'

'I mean it.' All at once she was conscious of a vast surge of relief. It was as if a heavy burden had been lifted from her shoulders. 'I've been thinking it over ever since Kevin——'

'Kevin! So that's who let you in on all this! Why can't he mind his own business?'

'He seems to think you are his business! Anyway, I would have heard all about it before long from someone else. Come on,' she smiled up at him in the gathering gloom, 'is it a deal?'

'I'll say it is! You can trust me not to go blabbing it all over the district, you can take my word for it.' A self-conscious grin touched his lips. 'You never know, seeing things won't be legally tied up for a time, anything could happen. You might have second thoughts, change your mind?'

Christine shook her head. 'Don't worry, I won't—come on, let's go and tell the others the news. I mean, about

your keeping on working here as manager for the new
owner!'

They turned and began to make their way down the
darkening slope. From somewhere over the hill came a
chorus of bird calls. 'What are those night birds?' Christine
asked, puzzled.

'Just the wekas.' He seemed to be scarcely listening.
'You know something, Christine? What gets me about all
this, apart from the big surprise package you've just
handed me, is you wanting to stay on here.'

She thought, if he says 'a girl like you' I'll scream loud
and clear. He didn't.

'But who knows, you might find the district around here
interesting at that. This is sheep country, Maori country.
Every little settlement is steeped in history and a lot of the
hills are old Maori *pas*—villages to you. If you happen to
go for native legends, history, all that stuff——'

'I like everything around here.' Why did her thoughts fly
to the dark enigmatic face of Kevin Hawke? Almost it was
worth giving up an inheritance to be able to prove to him
how mistaken he had been about her being able to persuade Laurie to continue on at Glendene as her right-hand
man. She could hardly wait to see his face when she told
him about it.

'Ben's car,' she wrenched her mind back to Laurie's
voice, 'at least take that for yourself.'

'Okay, I'll use it when I need it. We'll share it. There is
one thing I'd like to have, though——'

'Anything! Just say the word.'

'It's Trooper,' she said.

'Trooper?' He sounded incredulous. 'If that's what you
want ...'

'Unless you want to hunt him yourself?'

'I don't hunt, it's not my scene. It's just—well, Trooper's
not the sort of horse to be ridden by anyone but a strong
man. He's got an iron mouth. That's why Ben kept him as
a hunter, he wasn't even used for work on the farm, he was
too difficult to manage once he got out of a walk.'

'All the same, I'd like to have him. Maybe I'll even get around to riding him some day.'

Brave words, jeered the black goblin deep in her mind.

I will! I will! I won't always have this stupid phobia about taking a horse over a high jump. I'll get the better of it one of these days.

That'll be the rainy Sunday!

She smothered the tiny voice in her mind and concentrated on Laurie's apprehensive tones.

'He's yours, of course, but——'.

'I only want him because Uncle Ben was so attached to him,' she lied. 'If you could exercise him for me?'

'No problem.' He sounded abstracted. 'Look, there's the matter of money. At least let me——'

'No, no, no! I've got a little of my own saved up, enough to see me through the next few months, and the lawyer in London did advance me the fares. Don't worry, I'll get along. It's all settled.'

As they paused at the gate near the house Laurie caught her arm. 'Christine——' she knew he was finding difficulty in expressing his feelings, 'I haven't thanked you yet. I ... don't know how to.'

She smiled up into the serious young face. 'Uncle Ben's the one you have to thank, not me!'

When they reached the living room they found Ella seated knitting a garment and Fred, puffing at his pipe, was watching television.

Laurie said awkwardly, 'I've got some news for you two! Something that might make a lot of difference to your plans for looking around for another place. It's just that— well, Christine and I have been chewing things over and the upshot of it all is that I've decided to stay on.'

'As manager,' Christine put in brightly. Dropping to a low stool, she linked her hands around her knees. 'After all, as far as I can find out Laurie is the best man I could possibly find for the job—knowing the place so well, I mean, and having been here for so long.'

Never had she seen a couple look so completely taken

aback. Fred's mouth fell open, but no words came. After the first moment of stunned silence Ella's words came thick and fast. 'But, Laurie, you said that nothing on earth would induce you to do that, that you'd finished with Glendene for ever! Why, only a day or two ago when you went off to look for a farm position you said to me that money wouldn't buy you. You told me that no amount of extra wages would tempt you to stay on here. "I'm finished with Glendene for good," you said.' Ella's sharp brown eyes went from Christine's smiling face to Laurie's heightened colour. 'Whose idea was it?' she queried sharply. 'Yours or Christine's?'

Laurie looked more embarrassed than ever. 'We sort of cooked it up together.'

'I thought so.' What Ella thought was to Christine clearly expressed in the suspicious glance and tightly-pursed lips.

Laurie said awkwardly, 'You see, Ella, it was like this. I changed my mind——'.

'Or had it changed for you! If it wasn't money then all I can say is that you're mighty easily persuaded.' Christine could almost hear the words that hung in the air. What chance would he have, a country lad like Laurie, shy, in-experienced, unused to dealing with women, when it came to a lovely girl like this, a girl who had worldly experience, beauty and now that she had Ben's inheritance, wealth as well? Aloud she said appealingly, 'We thought, Laurie and I, we hoped, that it might make a difference to you and Fred. If you stay on too it will be just like old times——'

'That it won't!' Ella's steel knitting needles flashed fast and furiously. 'If you ask me it will never be the same again, not without Ben, not the way things are.' She gathered up her knitting and stood up, 'I told you, miss, we'll let you know our decision in the morning.' As she left the room, head held high and eyes stormy, Fred sent Christine a significant wink.

'She'll come round,' he said in his slow way, 'Give her

time and she'll see it's the best thing for us to stay on with you.'

Christine knew the battle was as good as won. She liked Fred and despite Ella's sharp tongue she almost liked the housekeeper. If only they didn't have this mistaken idea about her. If only she could convince them that pale gold hair and big dark eyes together with an ability to wear home-made garments with a careless elegance that had so often caused her to be mistaken for a fashion model were merely attributes she happened to have been born with. Try telling that to Kevin Hawke, jeered the goblin in her mind, and see how far it will get you!

Presently Fred went to his room to change into working garments while Ella and Christine sat on at the table. It seemed to Christine that Ella's tone had lost a little of its cutting edge. Could it be that the relief of knowing she was free to remain in the place she had come to regard as her own home had softened her attitude? I hope, I hope, she thought.

While she dried the dishes Christine said with assumed indifference, 'I met one or two of the local folk while you and Fred were away. Patrick came to see to his pony. He was a terrific help to me when Trixie got out of her paddock and headed non-stop for the road.'

Ella appeared unsurprised at the wandering habits of ponies. 'Stock are always getting out on to the road. They're lucky if they survive around here.'

'I know what you mean.' Christine dried a saucer. 'Someone else called in too, a man named Kevin Hawke. He came to my rescue, thank heaven, when the pig escaped.' She tried to make her tone nonchalant. 'Does he come here often?'

'Kevin? Oh, he's always in and out of the place.' Ella flicked a quick sideways glance in Christine's direction. 'Good-looking devil, isn't he? There aren't many girls around here who wouldn't give their ears for the chance of being Mrs Kevin Hawke.'

Christine felt a queer little thrill shoot through her. So he wasn't a married man!

'He's really someone around these parts,' Ella was saying, 'one of the biggest landowners in the country, prominent in the Hunt Club, a leader of the local polo team. And as to women ... you have only to look at him, I mean, there's something about him ... you can *feel* it!'

Christine schooled her voice to an indifferent note. 'I didn't notice.'

Liar! said the goblin. You can't get him out of your mind. Aloud she said, brightly, 'Goodness, he must be thoroughly spoiled by all the local female population.'

'He would be if he was any other man.' Ella paused, the dish mop held motionless in her hand, and Christine realised that the housekeeper was a woman who thrived on gossip. 'But Kevin doesn't bother much with any of them. Oh, a partner for the annual Hunt Ball in town, maybe, or someone to take along to a show now and again, that sort of thing. But as for getting seriously involved—after all,' she added darkly, 'he is a Hawke.'

'What do you mean?' To think she had mentally disapproved of Ella's gossiping ways, yet now she couldn't wait to hear the answer to her question.

'They don't settle down, the Hawke menfolk, until they're well into their thirties. At least that's the way it was with Kevin's grandfather and his father.'

'You mean they had a good look around first? Wild oats and all that?'

Ella shook her head. 'I wouldn't say that. All I know is that they make good husbands, the Hawke men, faithful to one woman all their life long.'

To Christine's relief Ella had apparently suspended her suspicious attitude towards Uncle Ben's niece in the interest of her subject. 'Andrea Stevenson now, she lives not far from the Hawkes' homestead in another old-established place up in the hills, she would like to be that one woman in Kevin's life, there's no doubt about that. She's been crazy about him ever since they were kids at boarding school coming home for the holidays. You can see the way she feels about him in the way she looks at him. He seems to like her well enough, but that's about as far as it goes.' Ella flicked the dish mop. 'Everyone knows the Hawke family. They've lived in the district for three generations. Kevin's grandfather came out from England in one of the early sailing ships, settled here and traded land from the Maoris. It was he who had the homestead built, a big house up in the hills a few miles from here. Their land runs for miles back into the hills, and luckily Kevin can afford to keep the place up. He's got quite a staff up there at Mata-Rangi—shepherds, mechanics, blacksmith, all living on the sheep station. Years ago the Maoris who used to work for Kevin called him "the King" and somehow the name has stuck.'

Christine felt hot with mortification. 'Goodbye, and thank you, Mr King.' How did one explain away a slip like that? She would be careful not to make that mistake again when next she saw him. Neither she vowed would she join the ranks of the local girls all longing to throw in their lot with the owner of the biggest sheep station around the district.

'Look,' Ella was saying, 'you can see the house from here.' She drew aside the curtains. 'Through the trees over on the hilltop, the big old two-storied place with the high shelterbelt of gum trees. There are quite a few places of the same type dotted around the district, but over the years the owners couldn't afford to keep the homesteads up and they've got more and more dilapidated. Some are empty or used to keep hay in. But there's nothing like that about Mata-Rangi. It's quite a show place. There was a TV documentary featuring the homestead just the other night. The camera crew came up from Wellington to make it. It was a programme showing what the old station homesteads in New Zealand look like.'

Christine was thinking of Kevin. He wore the summertime gear of the New Zealand sheep farmer, open-throated cotton shirt, tough work shorts, sturdy boots. How could she have guessed at his status among the friends and neighbours in this country district where he had grown up?

'Not that you'd hear anything of that from Kevin,' Ella seemed to tune in on her thoughts, 'he knows his job well and works alongside the men he employs.'

'Lucky Kevin.' Christine couldn't keep the wry note from her tones. At Ella's look of surprise she added quickly, 'I mean, he would always have other folk to help him with the work on his station.'

'But he has the responsibility of all,' countered Ella. 'He's made a study of sheep farming and he often takes trips overseas to attend wool conferences in other countries. At the wool sales in the city they say the fleeces from Mata-Rangi are always top quality, so clean that they fetch the highest prices. Kevin's brought in a lot of hill country and made it into good pastureland with the aerial top dressing. Of course it's expensive, but——'

'Evidently he can well afford it.' Christine couldn't understand what had got into her to make her so disparaging about the man. Well she did know the reason really, but she refused to allow herself to dwell on that!

She became aware of Ella's shrewd gaze. 'Now don't you go falling for him! There just isn't any future in it for you if you do! He's a bit of a loner where girls are concerned, in spite of being so attractive.' She added thoughtfully, 'Except for Wendy, of course. He sees quite a lot of her, especially in the last couple of years since her parents died and she moved into that big old house in town with only that deaf old aunt of hers for company. But then of course Wendy's different.'

'How—different?'

'She's just not like other girls of her age. She's delicate, she's never been strong. When she was a child she spent a lot of time going in and out of hospitals ... some bone disease, I believe, was the cause of the trouble. Nowadays she seems to have grown out of that except for a stiff leg, but she's still too frail to play any sports or to ride a horse, nothing strenuous. She tires easily. Oh yes, Kevin takes a lot of interest in her.'

Takes an interest. What a funny way, Christine mused, to describe the feeling between a man and a girl. Aloud, she murmured, 'Maybe he feels sorry for her.' Who was she trying to convince, Ella—or herself?

She brought her mind back to Ella's voice. 'She's had a lot of bad luck one way and another. Bad health, losing her parents, then having to see her old house sold up to pay the debts her father had incurred through speculating. It must be a lonely life for her in town with her aunt, but these days she spends a lot of time at the Hawkes' home. No wonder she thinks there's no man in the world like Kevin! But what he thinks about her—well, that's anyone's guess. Maybe he does just feel sorry for her. I wonder. Wendy will be twenty-one next month and his parents are putting on a party for her.' Ellen's voice took on a low, confidential note. 'Lots of the folk around here who know them both are expecting an engagement to be announced that night——'

'That's nice.' Why did Christine feel so oddly deflated?

'But I wouldn't be too sure about that. It's true that his parents are talking of making the property over to him and having a small house for themselves built down near the gates, but all the same ... after all, he could have a house-keeper.'

Christine reflected that he already had two girl-friends, both of whom—she forced her thoughts aside. What did it matter to her who Kevin Hawke married? Only in some curious way it did matter, tremendously!

CHAPTER FOUR

In the morning Christine awoke to an appetising tang of frying bacon mingled with the fragrant aroma of percolating coffee that wafted in from the kitchen. Before she could get up there was a tap at the door and Ella entered. 'Here you are,' she thrust a cup of tea towards Christine. 'I thought you might like this. Ben always had a cuppa first thing in the morning.'

'Thank you.'

Ella jerked the curtains aside and leaning forward Christine glimpsed the distant mountains clear-cut against the translucent blue of the sky.

Ella's reluctant gaze was taking in the satiny skin, the rumpled fair hair. 'You don't look a scrap different,' she admitted grudgingly. 'In the morning, I mean.'

'Should I?' Christine laughed up into Ella's slightly disgruntled face. Somehow today, freed of problems and that bothering conscience of hers, she felt like laughing. 'Did you imagine I was a make-up artist or that I wore a blonde wig? No, it's natural. When I was a kid I was one of those hideous children with white-coloured hair. I just hated always being called "Snowy", but I guess it was inevitable.'

'It's so pretty,' Ella murmured unwillingly.

Today, however, even Ella's uncompromising attitude failed to depress Christine. She sipped her tea and as the older woman continued to hover about uncertainly Christine decided to help her out. 'I hope you've decided to stay on with me,' she said in a friendly tone.

'We could do that, just to please you, of course.'

Christine tried to hide the twitch of her lips. 'Of course. Everything will go on just the same as ever. Your wages——'

Ella's small wry figure seemed to tighten. 'It wasn't the money that I was worrying about——'

'I know. It's me, isn't it? Look,' Christine said in her soft appealing voice, 'couldn't you forget about the owner bit? Pretend I'm a guest in the house? I won't be any trouble to you, I promise.'

'It's not you exactly,' Ella said awkwardly, 'it's just——'

'I know. The injustice of it all, but couldn't you overlook that side of things? Laurie and I had a good talk over it all, and if he feels happy about the way things are——?'

'Happy!' Ella stared towards Christine incredulously. 'Are you trying to tell me he's happy about staying on here to help *you*!'

'That's right. He seemed quite pleased with the arrangement.' Immediately the words were out Christine knew it had been the wrong thing to say.

Ella tossed her head. 'What do you expect?' she said sourly. 'He's a *man*, isn't he?'

It was no use, the woman was determined to put the wrong construction on Laurie's sudden change of heart, and honestly, Christine told herself as Ella left the room, you could scarcely blame her. Oh well, perhaps she could win her around in the end. You couldn't please everyone, especially when it came to a lost inheritance.

A little later, seated at the breakfast table with the others, she could see that Fred too was plainly puzzled by Laurie's attitude. His high spirits hardly matched the feelings of a man who, in direct contrast to all he had said to the contrary, was now pledged to work for the stranger who had supplanted him.

She mentioned the matter to him as they strolled together through the small gate and out to the garages where she had left her rental car. 'Know something? You nearly gave the game away, looking so excited and happy this morning.'

'Sorry about that.' He slanted her a shy boyish grin. 'It's a bit hard to hide your feelings when you're on top of the world like I am today!' A sudden anxiety shadowed his eyes. 'You haven't changed your mind? There's still time, you know. The appointment with the lawyer isn't until ten.'

She shook her head, the soft floss-like hair catching gleams of sunlight. 'Like I told you, I'm happy about the new arrangements if you are.'

'Happy?' His low contented laugh was his answer. 'If I could only tell you——'

'Don't try, I understand how you feel.' They had reached the cars garaged in the sheds. 'I could return the Mini when we go to town today. The rental firm said I could drop it in at the local depot. Then you could bring me back in Uncle Ben's car.'

'*Your* car, you mean.'

'Ours!' Laughing together, they went into the sheds and soon were manoeuvring the two vehicles through the wide entrance gate and out on to the roadway. Soon they were joining in the traffic speeding down the hill, pulling out to pass long sheep trailers and huge cattle trucks. Between gaps in the traffic she caught glimpses of towering green hills where an occasional old homestead built in an earlier era was visible through high shelterbelts of native trees. Down in the valley they swept past apple and citrus orchards, acres of grape vines turning to crimson in the late autumn sunshine, followed by plantations of yellow corn where the harvesters were busy.

Keeping the big car in sight, Christine followed Laurie as he passed the saleyards with their pens of sheep and cattle. So that, she told herself, was the destination of the traffic moving through the night past the farm on the hilltop. Presently she realised that hill properties were giving way to a flat area of suburban streets with their neatly-kept older homes interspersed with modern bungalows painted in fresh pastel tonings of yellow, blue, pink. She caught a glimpse of an expanse of blue sea, then Laurie was leading her down a long street where attractive stores and office blocks rose alongside white timber houses of an earlier era. Suddenly she became aware that her guide was turning in at a rental car garage and she turned too. The formalities in the depot were soon completed and leaving the big old car in a parking lot, they strolled together along the wide main street.

'So many flags.' Christine gazed upwards towards the bright colours fluttering from each store. Strings of pennants strung across the road at intervals fluttered in the breeze.

'A welcome for you,' laughed Laurie, 'though some folk would tell you it's all because of the Gisborne Centenary celebrations. When we've got things tied up with the lawyer I'll show you around the town. Actually it's quite historical. If you wouldn't be bored to death———'

'I'd love to see it!' Never before had she been interested in such matters, but there was something about the town that fascinated her. An air of prosperity, a leisurely friendly atmosphere. There were so many smiling faces and everyone appeared to be relaxed and to have time to chat with acquaintances and friends, even if it meant pausing amidst the shoppers moving along the footpaths.

'Here we are!' Laurie turned in at the door of a modern office block and Christine went with him up a flight of stairs and into a carpeted office. A friendly girl receptionist rose from her desk at their approach. 'Miss Rowles, Mr Stuart? Mr Selkirk is expecting you. Miss Rowles, will you come in please?' She was ushered into an inner sanctum where a tanned, keen-eyed man of middle-age rose to greet her.

'It's about Ben's will, I take it?'

It was amazing, Christine thought a little later, how little surprise the lawyer displayed on learning of her decision to gift the property to a man she considered to be the rightful inheritor. Then she realised that this was a small town, the lawyer had known her uncle and was acquainted with Laurie. No doubt he knew the truth of the matter and had no difficulty in accepting her decision.

'Um ... very commendable ... a nice gesture. That is,' he shot her a penetrating glance, 'if you've definitely made up your mind about this?'

'Oh yes, yes!'

Clearly, she reflected, he was endeavouring somewhat
unsuccessfully to conceal his own satisfaction at the news
of the transfer of Glendene to Laurie. Odd to think that an
inheritance of hundreds of acres of land, house, stock, outbuildings, could all be arranged by her signing the document the lawyer was taking from a file. 'You realise, of
course,' she brought her mind back to the brisk tones, 'that
this matter won't be finalised for five, maybe six months.'

'As long as that?' she faltered.

'I'm afraid so. These things take time and one can't hurry
them. There is a certain procedure to be followed, it all has
to go through the proper channels.'

'Yes, I see.' Disappointment showed in the droop of her
shoulders. She did see, only too well. Where now was her
plan to confront Kevin Hawke with the altered situation at
Glendene? Months and months to wait! But it couldn't be
helped. It would have been so gratifying to be able to tell
that authoritative, interfering, good-looking Kevin that he
had been entirely mistaken in his snap judgment of her,
that Laurie was now the owner of Glendene and she could
prove it. Telling him she had a plan to make the place over
to Laurie wouldn't be at all the same. She could well
imagine the glint of disbelief in those blue eyes were she to
acquaint him with her intention. She very much doubted if
he would believe her, for only hard facts would alter his
opinion of her. The prospect of enduring his scarcely veiled
contempt for six long months was daunting, but somehow
it had to be got through.

When she came out of the office Laurie leaped to his feet
and hurried towards her. 'Tell me, is it all okay?' He tried
to keep the tension from his voice.

'Fine. No trouble at all. He didn't even seem surprised at
the idea.' They went down the stairs together. 'But I don't
suppose anything surprises lawyers.'

He said in his diffident way, 'That's a relief. I—got the
idea you might have changed your mind about things.'

Christine said, surprised, 'Why do you say that?'

'Oh, I don't know. It was just—I got the idea you looked

a bit disappointed when you came out of the room back there.'

'Oh, that? It was just because it's going to take so long to get it all legally settled. Five, maybe six months before we can say we've really made the change-over.' She tried to banish Kevin's sardonic smile from her mind and smiled up at her tall escort. 'Think you can keep it to yourself for six months?'

An expression of relief crossed the blunt features. 'Honey, for a secret like that I could wait a lifetime! Anyway, what's a few months? It will go by before we know it!'

She said on a sigh, 'Maybe.'

'Right now,' he said on a jubilant note, 'I reckon this calls for a celebration.' Taking her arm, he piloted her through the sauntering crowd on the pavement and into a dimly-lighted restaurant. They seated themselves at a corner table and Laurie ordered a local wine. Then they studied the luncheon menu together.

'How about a fish meal?' Laurie suggested.

'Love it. Is it a local catch?'

'Couldn't be fresher. Caught in the harbour out there.'

Christine followed his gaze through the window to the nearby wharves where fishing boats were unloading their nets.

'Wait until you see the beaches around here. Waikanae is really something and it's still warm enough for swimming.'

With an effort she banished the sense of disappointment from her mind and smiled across the table at him. 'I can hardly wait.'

It was a meal that Christine enjoyed. Was it because she was no longer troubled by that bothering conscience of hers? A little later she waited in the lobby while Laurie settled the bill. All at once her heart gave an unaccountable lurch, because Kevin Hawke had come to join Laurie at the desk. Christine, a short distance away, stood watching—and listening.

'If I'd known you were coming into town today,' Kevin was saying, 'we could have joined forces.'

Laurie settled the account and pocketed the change. 'Didn't know myself until the last moment, but some urgent business came up out of the blue. Christine and I came in to town together to fix things up with the lawyer. Now we're celebrating!'

Kevin glanced towards her and Christine kept her brightest smile handy just in case, but there was no need. A brief nod of recognition and he had turned back to Laurie.

'Celebrating?'

'That's the idea!' Too late Laurie appeared to recognise his blunder. His open honest face was turning to a dark brick red. 'What I mean is we had to have lunch.'

'You said celebrating?' Kevin pursued relentlessly.

'Oh, that,' muttered Laurie, manifestly uneasy, 'just that we got things tied up legally and all that——' he caught himself up, 'that is, Christine did.'

Kevin stood very straight. His tone was cold and condemning. 'I got the idea you were opting out, looking for a manager's job up country?'

Laurie looked anywhere but into those cold accusing eyes. 'Changed my mind,' he mumbled, and added awkwardly, 'about staying on at Glendene, I mean.' He took a deep breath, appeared to get himself under control and said evenly, 'Christine put it to me that I carry on just the same as before and manage the place for her instead of Ben.'

To Christine the silence seemed to go on for ever. At last Kevin said briefly, 'I get it.'

It wasn't so much the words as the way in which they were said that chilled her. It was the moment of triumph she had longed for, yet she felt no elation. Instead she was feeling slightly sick in her midriff. He would think, of course he would, that——

A group of men had entered the lobby, farmers she guessed, judging by their weather-roughened faces and casual working gear of cotton shirts and drill shorts. 'Well, see you, Laurie——' Kevin turned away, then paused as the girl at the telephone desk called, 'Laurie? Are you Mr Stuart? I've just taken a message for you from your home. The vet rang there to say he'll be out your way and will be calling in right after lunch and could you return home as soon as you can?'

'Right!' Regretfully Laurie regarded Christine. 'I was planning to take you around a bit today, give you an idea of the town, but one of the stock ponies has gashed his leg pretty badly on some barbed wire and seeing the vet is on his way ... too bad you're going to miss out on having a city tour now that you're in town, unless——' To Christine's horror he was glancing towards Kevin. 'Hey, Kevin, do me a favour, will you?'

'No, no, not again! *Please*, Laurie, don't ask him! I'd rather go home now with you, honestly!'

Her plea fell on deaf ears, for already Kevin had left the group of men he had been with and was strolling towards them. Only his eyes didn't look friendly any more, they looked cold and disillusioned as though his friend had let him down. And guess who he held to blame for that! Right at this moment Christine would rather die than be shuffled on to the reluctant companionship of this man.

He said briefly, 'What's the problem?'

'No problem. Just if you've got a bit of time to spare how about doing me a favour? Show Christine around the town. She's new to the place and,' Laurie grinned engagingly, 'from what she tells me she's a tiger for local history and all that.'

'It doesn't matter,' she cut in. 'I really must get back too. There are oodles of things I have to see to at home.' It was no use. Kevin's eyes held the implacable expression that boded no particular interest in her likes or dislikes. *But he was interested in Laurie*. She only hoped he wasn't bent on escorting her around the town with the purpose of discovering the reason for Laurie's unexpected change of heart. As if it were anything to do with him! Desperately she made an attempt to escape his attentions. 'I'd really rather go another day.'

'No time like the present,' he told her blandly, and before she could make any further protest his hand was on her bare arm and he was guiding her firmly from the room.

Out on the street Laurie left them with a lift of his hand. 'Be seeing you, you two. No trouble for you to see Christine home, Kevin?'

'A pleasure.' Her lips tightened as she caught the terse note in his voice, but apparently Laurie noticed nothing unusual. Or more likely he was far too happy and excited today to take notice of anything. His world had changed to rose colour, hers to a dull grey.

She glanced up at Kevin, eyes bright with defiance. 'You don't have to do this!'

'You heard what the man said,' he returned coolly. 'My bus is parked two blocks down the street.' With the icy politeness that chilled her spirit he added, 'Where would you like to go?'

All at once her control snapped. 'Nowhere—with you! You don't really want to take me all around the place! So why pretend that you do? Laurie meant well when he asked you to do that, but he didn't understand. He doesn't know how you feel about me, but I do!' How could I help but know when you look at me with that accusing gleam in your eyes? she thought furiously.

They were standing facing each other, oblivious of the crowd milling around them. A small Maori boy, wide-eyed with wonder, paused to stare up at them.

'What makes you say that?' Kevin enquired coolly. 'I think it might be an interesting outing—well, enlightening, put it that way.'

Christine sighed exasperatedly and pushed away a strand of gold hair that was blowing across her eyes. 'I suppose you mean about what happened to make Laurie change his mind about me all of a sudden?'

'Something like that.'

'If you're so interested,' she snapped, 'why don't you ask him?'

'I would if I thought he'd let me in on it.'

The small boy, entranced, gazed from face to face. Then his mother swooped down on him. 'So that's where you are! I've been looking for you everywhere!' As he was borne away the childish tones floated back to them.

'Are they having a fight? I didn't know grown-ups had fights!'

'Come on,' Kevin muttered angrily, 'unless you want to keep on providing a sideshow for the locals.'

'Me? I like that! It's not me——'

'*Come on!*' He hurried her away at breakneck speed and she found herself all but running in an effort to keep up with his long strides. It was a relief to seat herself in the long red car, even though she had to endure his presence beside her. At least here they could discuss their differences in private. But what was the use? Clearly he had not the slightest intention of believing a word she said. He thumbed the starter and they moved in stormy silence along a wide attractive street.

As he guided the car through the traffic he murmured, 'Take a look at the boat up above your head.'

'I had noticed it.' Nevertheless she lifted her eyes to view a small model of a sailing ship that was suspended high above the crowded street.

'You don't know what ship that is?'

'No.' Why must he persist in making her feel inept and ignorant as well as hard and self-seeking?

'It's a model of Captain Cook's ship, the *Endeavour*. You can scarcely move a foot in the place without coming across something about the old boy. If you're wondering how the district got its name of Poverty Bay——'

'I'm not, actually.'

Relentlessly he pressed on as though she hadn't spoken. 'You can blame Cook for that too. He made the first European landing in New Zealand, but he left after three days. Seems the natives were hostile and he struck trouble.'

She shot him a swift sideways look. 'Like me!'

He took no notice whatever. 'Over there,' he indicated a white-capped headland standing out in bold relief in the bay, 'is Young Nick's Head.' A red light flashed on a traffic signal and he braked to a stop at an intersection. 'Aren't you going to ask me how it got its name?'

Perversely Christine remained silent.

It seemed, however, that nothing she could say or do could discourage him. 'Cook was voyaging in unchartered waters when his cabin boy called Nick sighted the headland. Cook made landfall here in——'

'October 9th 1769,' she cut in triumphantly. It was the one fragment of New Zealand history that remained in her mind from the glossary of facts she had run through before coming out here.

Kevin raised heavily marked eyebrows. 'My, my,' there was a tinge of respect in his ironic tone, 'you have been doing your homework after all. Oh well, that saves me from going into that!' The traffic lights changed to green and they went on down the street to sweep over a bridge spanning a wide river. 'Lots of rivers around here,' he told her in his maddening monotone. 'Gisborne is known as the "city of bridges" and what do you know? All the main streets are named after British statesmen.'

'Really?' She affected to stifle a yawn.

He threw her a sideways glance. 'Not interested in British history? How about Maori, then? Originally Gisborne was known as Turanga-nui-Kiwa——'

'What on earth does that mean?'

'I thought you'd never ask. It's "the great abiding place of Kiwi", Kiwi being one of the chiefs of the canoe that made landfall at the peninsula. Right here in the town——'

'You don't have to do this.'

'Don't interrupt!' He swung the car into a side street. 'I'm enjoying it!'

She said very low, 'You don't *look* as though you're enjoying it.'

'On our right,' they were passing a modern complex built

on the river bank, 'we have Kelvin Park Museum and Art Centre. Attractive design, wouldn't you say? No? Art means nothing to you?'

'It's not that——'

'It's quite a place, Gisborne. They call it the Sunshine City.' In spite of his ill humour a warm note of enthusiasm tinged his tones. 'Terrific climate, colourful history.' He threw her a mocking sideways glance. 'Too bad you're not interested in the Maori-pakeha bit, it's quite exciting—but then, of course,' his voice was deadpan, 'you won't be staying here, not for long.'

Christine made no answer. Let him figure that one out for himself!

They sped along a wide suburban street lined with timber bungalows painted in gay light colours, then took another bridge over a river. One thing, she comforted herself, at the speed at which they were taking in the city's attractions the sightseeing tour wouldn't take long to complete.

'It's quite a thing, the way of life in sunny Gisborne.' She brought her mind back to the deceptively bland tones. 'They call it the Sunshine City, and would you believe? It happens to be the first city in the world to greet the sun each day!'

She regarded him with suspicion, but his gaze was on the road ahead. Was he having her on? She could well imagine him doing just that.

'No, I wouldn't!' She stared determinedly out of the window, the breeze tossing the fine hair back from her forehead.

'No? It happens to be true all the same! Remember that, Christine, it will be something to tell the folks when you get home.'

'If it's true.'

'As if I'd put you wrong!' Kevin guided the vehicle towards a shopping thoroughfare. 'We are now heading for Waikanae beach.'

'A beach?' She couldn't help looking surprised. 'But this is a main street. I can't see——'

'You will in a minute. Patience, Christine.' They swept down a wide street beneath the fluttering coloured flags and soon they were leaving the busy city traffic behind. Presently he pulled up at a curve of coastline facing the bluest of blue seas where breakers washed gently up on a long unbroken expanse of firm white sand.

Christine sat very still. The roar of the surf was in her ears and the breeze cooling her hot cheeks was fresh with the salt tang of the sea. There was something about the unspoiled beauty of the vast sweep of coastline, grass blowing on the sandhills, the empty sea ... All at once she could feel the tensions and frustrations of the past few hours draining away. 'This fantastic beach,' she scarcely realised she was speaking her thoughts aloud, 'and no one swimming!'

'Wait until the weekend! Or after the shops and offices close this afternoon and the guys and girls come down for a quick dip. Too bad,' his sardonic glance sparked her to instant awareness, 'that you didn't bring a swimsuit with you today.'

'But I did!' Just for once in this unfamiliar territory where he was so knowledgeable and she found herself woefully ignorant she had an answer to his taunt. 'Laurie told me to bring one with me today. He said we'd come down to the beach while we were in town. Pity,' she made her tone off-hand, 'that you didn't think to bring along swimming trunks yourself!'

His triumphant glance should have warned her. 'Whatever made you think I didn't?' He looked so smug he was all but purring, she thought crossly. 'Tossed a pair in the back of the old bus last week and they're still there. What do you know? I threw in a couple of towels too. You're in luck!'

In luck! To be trapped into taking a swim with him! She wouldn't put it past him to duck her in the water, he was quite vindictive enough to be planning something of the sort. Not that she wouldn't get a lot of satisfaction from delivering a counter-attack!

He had got out of the car and was opening the passenger door. 'Changing sheds are a bit further along the beach.'

They made their way along the thick white sand and Christine turned into a timber building with low dividing walls and a shower-box at the end. When she came out Kevin was waiting for her, standing looking out over the rippling sparkling sea. Lean and muscular, his bronzed body was scarcely distinguishable from his tan-coloured swimming trunks. At that moment he swung around to face her and she saw a light leap into his eyes. It was gone in a flash, but it had been there, that appreciative masculine gleam. So he was human after all. In spite of his hostile attitude towards her at least he approved of her appearance. She felt a subtle satisfaction in the knowledge even though she couldn't help but be aware that even if she wasn't sun-tanned like every other girl in the place—well, not yet—a black bikini did a lot for supple slimness and a fair skin.

Kevin said in the lazy accents to which she was becoming accustomed, 'Aren't you worried about your hair?'

She was genuinely surprised. 'Goodness no! I never worry about that. It'll soon dry in this warm weather.'

He said no more on the subject and they strolled down over wet and shining sand. Did his friend Andrea have problems over her hair-set in salt water? she wondered. And why was she thinking of a girl whose name she had heard mentioned only once?

Then she was running into the water, pushing her way through flying spray and curling white-topped breakers. Even the remembrance of Kevin Hawke's ill-humour and abrasive comments couldn't dim her feeling of exhilaration as she made her way through salt water that was both invigorating and refreshing. All at once a moving wall of green surged towards them, knocking Christine off balance and sending her floundering beneath the wave. Laughing and breathless, she picked herself up and ignoring Kevin's outstretched hand she made her way out beyond the tossing waves. Then they were swimming out in the deep. She was glad that in the water she was fairly proficient, her effortless crawl taking her swiftly over the restless sea.

'Hey, you're quite a swimmer!' There was a note of genuine surprise in Kevin's voice, but Christine scarcely noticed his call. She was treading water waiting for the arrival of the white-crested comber that was surging towards her.

'Come on!' Before she could remonstrate he had taken her hand in his and together they threw themselves on the swiftly moving breaker to be swept in to shore. Again and again they returned to the deep to toss themselves on the great swells that carried them towards the shallows but now there was no linking of hands. Christine made certain of that. One didn't join forces with the enemy.

In this sun-burnished world where there was only the wild flurry of the waves, the tossing spray and the warm sands of the shallows she lost count of time. At last they waded ashore. Christine wrung out her wet hair, then spread out her towel on the warm sand and dropped down, hands linked behind her head and eyes on the translucent blue bowl above. 'I could stay here for hours.'

'You'll be sorry if you do!' He was standing at her side looking down at her. 'With that fair skin of yours, you'll burn! I'd take it gradually if I were you.'

'I suppose so.' Reluctantly she got to her feet and picked up her towel. She didn't burn as a rule, but in this hot sun on the beach ... Why was he always right? Well, nearly always.

'Of course, if you want to be a cot-case for the rest of the week?'

So they were back to square one, she thought on a sigh. The time spent together in the spray-tossed sea had been a respite, that was all. As they made their way over drifts of sand her thoughts ran riot. If he allowed himself he would like me. Put it this way, he likes the way I look. That's exactly the reason why he won't let himself get personally involved. He's made up his mind that just because I happen to be rather attractive I've deliberately entrapped Laurie with my feminine wiles. He's determined I'm not going to do the same where he's concerned. Don't worry, Mr King—sorry, Hawke, I wouldn't bother even if I could. Why should I? All the same, you know something? It might be easier than you think!

When she was dressed once again in yellow shirt and blue jeans she wrung out her wet bikini and went out into the sunshine, conscious all the time of a delightful sense of relaxation.

Kevin was strolling towards the car and she hurried over the drifts of sand to join him. 'That swim was super!' She supposed she owed him something for giving her his time, even though he was taking her around city and surrounds against his inclinations and only because of his friendship with Laurie. She added somewhat reluctantly, 'And the sightseeing trip has been great too.'

He saw her seated in the car. 'You haven't set eyes on half of the district yet,' he told her in his deceptively mild accents. 'There are all the bays up the coast to visit, the hot springs at Morere, the Falls——'

'Thank you,' she said hastily, 'but a look around the town will do me for a start.'

'I'll tell you what we'll do,' he reached a hand towards the starter, 'I'll take you for a run up Kaiti Hill.' Presently they were sweeping towards the wharves to take a winding path up a bush-clad slope. Above them a white stone obelisk stood out against a backdrop of sombre native greenery.

Christine sent him a swift glance. 'Don't tell me, I'll tell you! The obelisk marks the spot where Cook first set foot on New Zealand soil?' Thank heaven a few odd facts culled from her brief study of the country had stayed with her.

He didn't even trouble to turn his head. 'You're learning fast.'

The next moment she was leaning forward eagerly in her seat, her fascinated gaze fixed on the crossed beams of a carved Maori edifice. Forgetting all about trying to appear uninterested in her surroundings, she said eagerly, 'Is that a Maori meeting house? Is that what the name means—Poho-o-Rawiri, meeting house?'

He nodded. 'The largest one in the country.'

Once again she regarded him doubtfully. 'Are you sure?'

'Of course I am.' He braked to a stop outside the building. 'Let's take a look inside, shall we?'

They strolled over the grass towards the great thatched hut, then paused at the entrance, gazing up at the crossed beams overhead. 'The beams are a good example of the old Maori patterns in carving,' Kevin told her. 'You'll see the same thing inside the meeting house in the panelling too.' He took her arm lightly, carelessly, so why did his touch send an electric excitement pulsing through her senses? He of all men! Her thoughts were in a tumult. What was happening to her? Could it be that hate affected one in the same way as love? But she imagined she had been in love with Jason, yet never had she felt this wild mixed-up excitement when she had been with him.

Alone with Kevin in the dimness of the thatched hut, all at once the ordinary everyday world seemed far away. Was it his voice, so deep and low and vibrant, that cast the spell?

'It tells a story, all this carving and the panelling designs. The old Maori tribes didn't have any written language, they relied on songs and stories passed on from father to son and all their carving designs carried a meaning—you're not listening, are you, Christine?'

It was very still, only the gleaming blue-green pawa shell eyes of the carved crouching gods seemed alive. The masculine magnetism against which she unconsciously had been struggling since their first moment of meeting—she could almost *feel* it—was sweeping everything else from her mind. There was something about his nearness . . . Her face lifted to his, then he was pulling her roughly towards him. She felt herself swept into his arms. A sudden dizzy rapture filled her heart and almost without her volition her arms slid around his neck and her lips clung to his.

The moment shattered as he released her so abruptly that she all but fell. She fought for control, but her voice came out with a betraying tremor. 'Why—did you do that?'

There was a contained anger in his eyes. 'Just proving a theory of mine, that's all.'

A strange emotion took hold of her so that she wanted to cry. She said very low, 'What do you mean?'

He said coolly, disinterestedly, 'You know what I mean. Oh, I'm willing to admit you can get everyone else around here eating out of your hand. Not me!'

The words cut deep and the hurt was more than she would have believed possible. 'You think I let any man kiss me, any stranger at all?' Humiliation swept her and the hot colour flooded the transparent skin of her cheeks. 'You've made up your mind that was why Laurie changed his mind all of a sudden about staying on at Glendene with me?'

There was steel in his voice. 'It's fairly obvious, isn't it?'

'It's not true, what you're thinking!' Her eyes blazed with indignation and hurt. 'Laurie had other reasons for doing what he did!'

'Such as?'

At his sceptical glance she was silent. Let him think what he pleased of her. He would find out before many months had passed how mistaken he had been in his snap judgment of her. For a long moment she was tempted to fling the truth in the dark mocking face, but what was the use? Promises, good intentions would mean nothing to him. Nothing less than legal proof would convince him, and until matters were settled she remained the owner of Glendene. Besides, a stubborn sense of pride forbade the explanation of her motives to this interfering stranger.

'I suppose,' she said in a low tone, 'that was the whole purpose of your escorting me around today?'

'Not quite.' She didn't ask him what he meant. There was no point in inviting further insults. Instead she heard her own voice sounding strangely like that of a lost and frightened child, 'Let's go home now, do you mind?'

The silence persisted all the way back to town. Christine could feel her cheeks burning with humiliation. She was bitterly ashamed of that other part of her that had betrayed her into her ardent response to Kevin's traitorous kiss. Well, she stared unseeingly out of the window, it wouldn't happen a second time. She wouldn't even see him again, not unless circumstances beyond her control forced her into a meeting. She dragged her heavy thoughts back to the present.

'Okay with you if we make one more stop? I promised Wendy I'd pick her up and take her home for the weekend.'

How could he speak in that casual tone to her when all the time . . . She choked back the anger and tried to make her voice steady. 'I don't mind.' Under her breath she muttered, 'Not that it would make the slightest difference to you if I did!'

Wendy—the name rang a bell in her mind. Of course, the girl, according to Ella, in whom Kevin took 'a lot of interest', whatever that might mean. Even if Wendy did suffer from indifferent health she would no doubt be clever and sophisticated. A girl would have need of those qualities to cope with Kevin Hawke and his high-handed ways.

They swept along a street lined with older houses, to cross yet another bridge, then Kevin was braking at the gates of a white-painted villa-type dwelling with wide verandahs and lawns running down to the river banks below.

'Wait here, will you, Christine, I won't be long!' He was out of the car and striding up the gravelled path. Presently two figures came into sight around the corner of the house.

Wendy—such a gay little name for the extremely thin plain girl who was leaning heavily on Kevin's supporting arm. Their progress was slow, and ever sensitive to another's distress, Christine averted her gaze from the limping figure.

A few moments later as Kevin helped Wendy into the car, Christine amended her initial impression of the girl's plainness. Pale, thin, a little stooped because of her lameness, but no girl could be called ordinary with those great grey eyes that seemed to shine with light and expression.

'Sorry to crowd you,' she murmured as she squeezed in beside Christine, 'it's this darn leg of mine. I always have to have the front seat, it makes it easier for me to get in and out of the car. That's right, isn't it, Kevin?'

He closed the door and came around to the driver's seat. 'Why not?' He flashed a smile in Wendy's direction. 'There's swags of room for three—so long as they all get on well together.'

Now just what did he mean by that remark? Christine wondered. The next moment she told herself she was becoming stupidly imaginative where he was concerned. Come to think of it, one way and another he was scarcely ever out of her thoughts! Pressed close against his lean muscular body, she tried to move away a little. He chuckled, a mellow sound deep in his throat. 'No need to be afraid of me, Christine!'

She threw him an indignant glance. How could he know that his nearness was rattling her composure, making her more than ever aware of him? As if he'd care if he did! Thinking of the man at her side brought back the memory of his kiss and with it came a hot sense of mortification. She had to force herself to concentrate on Wendy's light tones.

'Don't tell me, Kevin, let me guess!' Wendy had a happy laugh almost like a child's careless merriment. Indeed, there seemed to Christine to be a childish innocence about the girl, or could it be her own imagination? She was smiling towards Christine. 'You're Ben's niece? The girl who came out from England to take over Glendene?'

'Right first time!' With a sense of relief Christine realised that here at last was someone who wasn't prepared to dislike her at sight because of circumstances over which she had no control—well, until today!

'I've often been over to see Ben,' Wendy confided. 'Kevin took me to Glendene sometimes when I've been staying at his place.'

'You knew my uncle well, then?' Christine murmured for something to say.

'Oh yes! Ben was always interested in my spinning and weaving and Ella liked to see the toys and slippers and things I make from the fleeces.' She smiled happily. 'I have to go to Kevin's home every now and again to see how the black sheep are getting along. He breeds them specially for me, don't you, Kevin?'

'They're yours, honey, you know that.'

So he could be nice, it seemed. Probably he showed this side of his nature to everyone except the girl from England. It wasn't *fair*! Christine pulled a face in his direction and realised the next moment that he had caught her reflection in the long overhead mirror. The slight lift of black brows told her all too plainly that he hadn't missed her defiant gesture.

To tide over the moment of awkwardness she said to Wendy, 'Tell me, is it just the black fleeces that you use in your work?'

'Goodness, no! I like the dyed fleeces to work with too, they're such gorgeous colours, violet and pink and red and blue. I've made ever so many pairs of moccasins, given them to just about everyone I know. Now I'm working on knee-boots, wool-lined and all.' Again the childish trill of laughter. 'Kevin says he'll wear them when I've made them, but,' she dropped her voice to a confidential note, 'I think he only tells me that to keep me happy.'

'Who says so?' came the indignant masculine tones. 'You make 'em, I wear 'em! It's a deal.'

The girl's face fell. 'I've never made them before. They might not be good enough——'

'They'll be terrific! I wouldn't mind betting that Miss Rowles takes a pair back with her for her boy-friend when she takes off again for home.'

'I haven't any——' Christine stopped short. She didn't

have to fill him in with details of her personal life, and why must he persist in reminding her of her return to England? Probably, she thought on a sigh, because he couldn't wait to be rid of her.

'When are you going back home, Miss Rowles?' Christine became aware of the light sweet tones. 'Maybe if I had time I could make you something really nice to take with you.'

'You'll have time,' Christine promised. She refused to give Kevin the satisfaction of knowing the intended length of her stay here.

He was swinging the car into the driveway of Glendene when Wendy leaned towards her. 'It's been super meeting you.'

Conscious of Kevin beside her, Christine said quickly, confusedly, 'We'll have to get together another day.'

'Oh yes, we will!' The pale face lighted up. 'Maybe Kevin could bring me here one day or take you over to his place. Not tomorrow, though, that's the day of the Opening Hunt that's being held at Ben's—I mean your place. Isn't that right, Kevin?'

He nodded briefly, braking to a stop at the small gate where a narrow path led down to the house. 'That's the arrangement.' His voice hardened as he swung around to face Christine. 'If that's okay with you, Miss Rowles?'

The cold formality of his tone struck her like a blow.

'Of course ... I didn't know.' She managed to collect her thoughts. 'Laurie told me that Uncle Ben belonged to the Hunt Club——'

'Something you wouldn't be interested in?'

She prayed he would not have noticed her momentary hesitation and placed his own construction on it. 'No, no, not me!'

'Pity. You could have given us a line on how things are done over in England.'

Now, however, she had got herself firmly in hand. 'Oh, I'm sure you know all about that already.' Gathering up her bag, she slipped the strap over her shoulder. 'Goodbye,' she avoided his gaze, 'and thanks for doing your duty today!'

Briefly she wondered what he would have said had he been truthful enough to admit how he *really* felt about being forced to escort her around the town. One could scarcely term such a rushed trip 'sightseeing'.

'My pleasure,' he said, tight-lipped.

Just in time Christine forced back the rejoinder that sprang to her lips. 'No doubt.' For hadn't his pleasure been his moment of revenge taken in the shadows of the thatched Maori hut? As Kevin reversed down the slope she stood looking after him, waving to Wendy whose head was thrust from the open window. She *must* put from her mind that moment in the meeting house.

CHAPTER FIVE

As she moved towards the house Christine's eyes lifted to a green slope where Laurie and Jan stood beside a man wearing a white coat. A bay horse was tethered to a fence nearby. So the vet was still here?

She strolled up the rise to join them and as she neared the group became disconcertingly aware of Jan's hard resentful stare. One thing was for sure, she thought on a sigh, the other girl wasn't going to forgive her for coming here in a long while. The next moment she became aware of a look of warm interest from the vet. He was a short thick-set young man with a trimmed black beard and a merry twinkle in his eyes. 'Hi,' he grinned towards Christine as introductions were made, 'I was hoping if I stuck around long enough I'd meet you. That I should be so lucky!' He had an infectious chuckle. 'Laurie's been telling me about you, but he didn't really—I mean, you've got to see to believe.'

She felt her heart lift a little. After the gruelling time Kevin had put her through, frank admiration even from a man as young and lighthearted as Gavin Massey was something she could well do with right now. She smiled back at him, 'I take it you're the local yet?'

'Junior partner,' he corrected her, 'very junior, actually. There's a hell of a lot to learn here. This is horse country, a line I haven't had much experience in, coming from the city, but I'm getting there. Thing is, just at present I cop all the uninteresting jobs like checking up on this fellow,' he indicated a wound on the horse's fetlock, 'just a gash, though it looks nasty. He'll be as good as new in no time at all.'

Laurie had not missed Christine's expression of surprise. He said with a grin, 'Gavin's not really as slow as all that. He hasn't taken hours to make the diagnosis. He got held up and only arrived here twenty minutes ago. As things worked out,' he murmured regretfully, 'I could have escorted you around the high spots of the town after all.'

Jan, her eyes dark with suspicion, glanced from Laurie to Christine.

'It didn't matter,' Christine said for the other girl's benefit. 'Your friend Kevin gave me a quick look around the place and I got a good idea of it all. The main impression I got about Gisborne was that it's Maoriland.' Out of a corner of her eye she saw Jan relax.

'If I'd had the chance,' Gavin's gaze was riveted on Christine's face, her cheeks pink from the touch of the sun on Waikanae beach, 'it wouldn't have been a quick run-around. I'd have made the trip last all day and half the night.'

She twinkled up at him. 'That's what you think! Anyway, I might have had other things to do, like taking a look around here.'

Laurie took her up promptly. 'Why not now?'

'Love to.'

He hesitated for a moment. 'It's easiest to go on horse-back, though. You did say you've done a bit of riding?'

'Yes, I——'

'You could ride one of the stock ponies. You won't have

to bale out on one of them and they can take the steepest hills, no trouble. They're born and bred here.'

'That will suit me.'

Gavin's face fell. 'I suppose,' he said ruefully, 'I can't blame you for taking off. I know what I'd feel like if some-one had left me a property—stock, house, the lot. I couldn't wait to take a look at everything. Guess you feel the same way.'

'Something like that.' She caught Laurie's eye and he sent her a conspiratorial wink, a wink that unfortunately was intercepted by Jan's watchful eye. She said quickly, 'I'll come along with you.'

'Right.' Laurie appeared to notice nothing amiss. 'You can give me a hand to saddle the horses.' He added in his slow diffident way, 'Christine hasn't got around to learning the ropes yet.'

'And she never will.' Only Christine caught Jan's low words.

'I'd better get cracking too,' Gavin murmured reluct-antly. His lingering glance towards Christine signalled an unmistakable, 'Worse luck!' He came to stand beside her. 'I'll ring you,' he said, 'you might like to do a show with me in town one night?'

She smiled, 'I might.'

When he had gone she went into the house to change. Fortunately she had brought with her a pair of worn riding breeches that she had been in two minds whether or not to throw away. Maybe people here wouldn't feel so resentful towards her if she looked more 'ordinary', but in her heart she knew that appearances were against her. A cloud of silky honey-gold hair, a complexion that looked like a make-up advertisement but wasn't—why, even Kevin Hawke had thought she looked artificial. She snatched up an open-throated white T-shirt and pulled it over her head. As if his opinion of her mattered!

A comb ran swiftly through her hair and she was ready. When she reached the stables she found Laurie and Jan were already carrying saddles out to the quiet-looking hacks who stood blinking in the afternoon sunshine. She knew somehow that riding over the hills wouldn't worry her, not on one of these sturdy workaday mounts. Ridiculous though she knew her fears to be, it was the prospect of taking a horse over the high jumps that sent her nerves sheering away in blind terror. Who knows, she told herself, maybe the ride over the sheep farm today might help to dispel the block in her mind.

As Laurie helped her up on her mount she asked, 'What's his name?'

'That's Brownie.'

She laughed, 'I might have known!'

She patted the thick neck, then urged the bay forward. It was a joy to be in the saddle once more, to know once again the mingled odours of leather and horseflesh. They reached the first gate with Jan in the lead and she opened it and closed it again when the others had passed through the opening. Christine longed to push her horse to a canter, but just in time she remembered she was supposed to be a novice rider.

They turned along a pathway and presently Laurie drew rein at the open doors of a hutlike building raised two or three feet above the ground. She pulled her mount to a stop beside him. 'Is this the woolshed?'

He nodded. 'This is where the action is. Everything to do with the care of the sheep and the harvesting of the wool. This is all part of it,' he indicated the holding pens, the water race, the sheep dip and open sheds housing tractor and fencing wire.

Christine murmured, 'There's such a lot to know——'

'But you don't need to learn about it,' Jan cut in. 'You'll have nothing to do with the work of the place, not unless you want to. Laurie will see to all that.' Her tone implied, 'You have all the pleasure and profit of owning Glendene, while all he has is work and responsibility.'

'I guess so.' Christine slipped to the ground. 'If you'll wait for me—I'll take a look inside.' She peered in the wide open doors of the great shed with its presses and high rafters and floor shiny with the oil of the fleeces.

'Hello there!' Fred, wielding a massive broom, appeared from the shadows. 'I'm cleaning up here ready for the Hunt breakfast tomorrow. Do you hunt, by any chance, Miss Rowles?'

'Not me,' she flashed him a bright smile, 'and it's Christine, remember?'

'Oh well, I don't suppose you'll mind giving Ella a hand to carry out the food.' He gestured towards a huge scrubbed table near the opening. 'She carries all the stuff from the house down here, so everything's ready when the riders turn up. She puts on quite a spread, does Ella. Hot food, savouries—you name it, she supplies it. Ben, he always used to see to the drinks, beer in the hot weather, whisky and sherry in the cold part of the winter. Mind you, the women riders usually bring along a plate when they come.'

'A plate?' She eyed him in bewilderment. 'Whatever for?'

He chuckled at her puzzled expression. 'Of eats, love. It all helps. I doubt, though, if that will happen tomorrow. Everyone around here knows that Ella's just about the best cook in the district. She takes a pride in her reputation that way. You'll see what I mean tomorrow.'

Laurie held her mount steady while she pulled herself up to the saddle. 'Fred was in there cleaning up for the Hunt breakfast tomorrow,' she told him.

'That's right,' Laurie confirmed as the three rode abreast over the dried grass. 'I'm putting some spars on the fences for the Hunt tomorrow. The opening Hunt of the season is always held at Glendene, it's a sort of tradition.'

'Things are a bit different this year,' Jan said sharply. 'Doesn't it all depend on Christine? I had the idea that riders had to get the owner's permission before they can hunt over a property.'

Darn the girl! Christine thought exasperatedly. Jan seemed bent on making things unpleasant for her. Not that one could blame her in a way. Christine forced away the resentful thoughts and said quietly, 'Of course it's all right.

All I want is for things to go on in the same way as they always did.'

Jan made no reply and they went on up the slope. All at once Christine noticed the absence of the white pony in the small paddock.

Laurie followed her gaze. 'Patrick came and collected his pony this morning, while you were in town,' he explained. 'It was only here for a while to be educated before he started riding it.'

'Well, at least Trooper's here.' They had come in sight of the big strapping grey moving restlessly along the fence line. 'It's all right, old boy,' she sent the thoroughbred a mental message, 'I know how you must feel, penned up in your paddock on a gorgeous day like this with everyone else out over the hills. Don't worry though, have patience for a little while and *I'll* be riding you to the hunt again— one of these days.'

As they followed the worn sheep tracks that circled the steep slopes she realised that her sturdy mount was well accustomed to the route. She and Jan waited while Laurie dismounted in order to fix a spar to a barbed wire fence running across the hillside. All the time as they rode on, Christine realised, Laurie was alert to the possibility of the smallest gap in the long line of boundary fences. As they went on steers milled nervously around them, to gallop away in sudden panic and huddle together in a black mass.

At length they reached the summit and drew rein. Christine sat motionless, gazing over fold after fold of cleared hills, darker green in the gullies where feathery pungas, nikau palms and tall native trees ran up between the slopes.

'The cleared strip over there,' Laurie told her, pointing to an airstrip, 'is for the planes when we get the crop-dusters to drop their load over the far hills.'

Now at last she could see the sheep, dotted as thickly as balls of cotton wool as they nibbled the green slopes. 'All those sheep,' she marvelled aloud, 'and only you, Laurie, to look after them all.'

'Why not?' As usual Jan seemed determined to let slip no opportunity of reminding Christine that she was a usurper here. 'He's been doing that for ages, and if it hadn't been for a stupid accident——'

Laurie sent her a warning glance. 'Cool it, will you?'

Jan subsided with a sulky stare. After a moment she muttered resentfully, 'It's about time that someone came right out and told her——'

'There's no need,' said Christine quietly. 'I know all about Uncle Ben intending Laurie to have Glendene.'

Jan was open-mouthed with astonishment. 'You—know?'

'I've known since I first arrived here.'

'Hold the rein for me, will you, Jan?' Laurie looked acutely embarrassed. With a murmur of putting some stays on the fences he began to climb down the hillside.

Christine could tell from the other girl's angry expression that Jan wasn't going to give in without a struggle. 'Well, I think you're awfully lucky to get Laurie to stay on and work for you. Lots of men *in his position* wouldn't have kept on with you, not for any amount of extra pay.'

'It wasn't the money.'

Pain and suspicion mingled in Jan's searching glance. 'What's that supposed to mean?'

'Not what you're afraid of! It was just that I don't know the first thing about sheep farming. Laurie agreed to stay on and help me out, that was all.'

Something in Christine's clear-eyed gaze must have got through to Jan. She said reluctantly, 'I suppose it wasn't your fault, what happened here.'

'Not really.' She caught sight of Laurie coming over the rise a short distance away. 'Let's go and meet him, shall we?'

As they moved forward Christine reflected that though it wasn't much, at least she had made a start in the way of good relations.

When they reached Laurie, they found him gazing down a steep grassy slope. One would need to be an experienced rider, she mused, to hunt over such high hills as these. Kevin Hawke would be used to such difficult terrain, of course, having lived in the district all his life.

Laurie seemed to tune in on her thoughts. 'Kevin will be bringing Andrea out with him tomorrow. She's only just got back from her European trip, but she won't miss the first hunt of the season, I bet.'

'She wouldn't miss anything that was going that would give her the chance of being with Kevin,' Jan said shrewdly. 'It's just too bad for Andrea that he's not the marrying kind.'

'Don't be too sure,' Laurie flicked her a warm glance. 'That's what the guys used to say about me, then I met you, and that was it!'

Jan's face lighted up with sudden radiance. 'That's right, whatever happens, we've got each other.'

Feeling forgotten in an alien land, Christine prodded her mare's broad sides with her heels. The next moment they were taking one of the sheep trails that threaded the hillside. When they reached the flats once again she forgot everything else as she broke into a canter. The wind flew past her ears and about her was the fresh tang of the countryside. She was getting back to her old self, feeling relaxed and happy in the saddle. Before long she would have her courage back and take these barbed wire jumps across the hillside—of course she would!

Presently the other two riders joined her and as their mounts slowed to a walk, Christine said to Jan, 'If Ella has so much extra work to do tomorrow, perhaps she would be glad of a hand with it.'

'I doubt it.' But she didn't sound quite so antagonistic, Christine thought hopefully.

'She takes a terrific pride in her baking, likes to do it all herself. All the same,' for the first time in their brief acquaintance Jan seemed to be speaking naturally, 'I daresay she'll let you help in other ways, carrying plates over to the woolshed, making tea and coffee and all that. Why don't you ask her?'

In spite of Jan's somewhat offputting manner the other girl's tone was careless, almost as if she were chatting with any other girl. Wryly Christine reflected that if just one person here changed their attitude towards her and became really friendly she would count it a victory. Apart from Laurie, that was. You couldn't count him, not when the slightest hint of friendliness on his part was viewed by Jan with instant suspicion. Oh dear, what a mix-up it all was, and why was it that 'one person' evoked in her mind the dark enigmatic face of Kevin Hawke?

Back in the stables with the others she lifted the saddle from Brownie's broad back and wiped the sweating horse down with a towel. Then hanging the bridle on one of a row of hooks on the wall above her head she went to the outside washroom to wash her hands.

In the kitchen she found Ella busily preparing refreshments for the next day's meet. The room was filled with aromatic odours of baking and the long sink bench was stacked with pizza pies filled with bacon, tomato and spaghetti and still hot from the oven.

'Oh, hello, Ella——'

'Don't touch those! I want them for tomorrow!' Ella turned a face flushed from the heat of the range.

Guiltily Christine replaced the cloth covering steaming ginger gems. 'They look so tempting.'

'Oh well, you can have one, I suppose,' Ella offered grudgingly. In a milder tone she said, 'Did you have a good look around the town?'

Christine felt relieved that the housekeeper appeared to be getting over her initial attitude of resentment. After all, one could scarcely go on living in the same house with someone and keep on hating them for ever.

'Oh yes,' she took the opportunity of making a friendly approach, 'I expect Laurie told you he got called back here to see the vet, so he asked a friend of his to run me around. Kevin Hawke, his name is.'

'He's a bit more than a friend, second cousin or something of the sort. Laurie was left an orphan when he was quite young and Kevin's parents brought him up. That's where he got his love of farming in the first place.'

So that, Christine mused, explained Kevin's red-hot resentment against her over a matter that was really none of his concern. It was dreadful, she was fast becoming as gossipy as Ella, but she couldn't seem to help herself. 'On the way back from town we picked up the girl you told me about—Wendy. Kevin was taking her to stay at his home for a time.'

Ella nodded. 'Oh yes, the Hawkes do all they can for her, have her up to stay with them a lot. She'll be staying there for good one of these days, I wouldn't wonder. They're all very good to her, especially Kevin.'

Especially Kevin! Was that what he wanted in a wife? A blind hero-worship? A childlike devotion? No wonder, she flinched away from the memory of the incident at the meeting house, he had been at pains to show her exactly how he felt about her.

She wrenched her mind back to Ella's voice, asking, 'Where's Jan?'

'Out in the stables with Laurie. She said she had to go home early and only came over here with a message from her father.'

'That'll be the day!' snorted Ella. 'She comes over to see Laurie every chance she gets, and the way things are now,' she added significantly, 'she'll be here more than ever to keep an eye on him.'

Christine said quickly, 'The property is so big, isn't it? From the top of the hill where Laurie took me we could see for miles and miles.'

'There are lots of big properties around here. Glendene is nothing compared with the Hawke station.'

Christine did not want to hear about the Hawkes with their name and their lands and their precious Kevin who seemed to think that being master of an old homestead in an island in the Pacific over a thousand miles from anywhere meant being a sort of king. There she went, thinking of him again. He was always in her mind. It must be because of his unforgivable treatment of her today. She wrenched her thoughts aside and said to Ella, 'From what I've been hearing you're going to be awfully busy tomorrow. Could I help? What about sandwiches? Maybe I could make those fat stacked ones with lots of fillings?'

'You could do that.' To her surprise Ella sounded almost friendly. 'I've got scones made in the deep-freeze, but they'll need cream and jam put on them and I like the sandwiches to be made fresh.'

Christine took a sneaky advantage. 'They tell me you've got a reputation in the district for the spreads you put on here on Hunt days?'

It worked. There was a brightening of the small face, a happy lift of a neat head. 'Really? Oh well, I do my best, and I do enjoy baking.'

'I can see that.' Christine glanced along the plates of muffins, the date loaves and fruit cake. 'Will the Hunt crowd really eat all of this?'

'You'll be surprised,' Ella said with satisfaction, 'at what they can put away, after all that riding and jumping over the hills.' A shadow crossed her face. 'It seems so odd not getting Ben's white stock starched and ironed, sending his hunting jacket to the cleaners. And Trooper, I don't know what's going to happen to him. Ben always boasted that he owned the best hunter in the country, and Kevin Hawke thought the same. He offered to buy Trooper from Ben time and time again, but Ben always said he would never sell. You see, he'd bred and trained Trooper himself and he knew he would never find another thoroughbred to match him. Not that he's a young horse any longer, but he's strong and sound with a great heart. Ben used to say that he'd never known Trooper to refuse a jump when he took him to the hunt.' She sighed. 'Oh well, times change, and perhaps you'll decide to——'

'Never!' Christine could scarcely believe the assertive tones were her own. 'He won't be sold, you can be sure of that!' She added silently, and especially not to Kevin Hawke! I only wish he would make me an offer for

Trooper. What a chance it would be for me to even the score!

The mail brought a letter from her mother. She and her husband were touring through the Lake District. To Christine her mother seemed happy and content, which was more than she could say for herself. She sat for a long time pen in hand, finding difficulty in writing of her experiences in a new and unknown land. There was so much to say, yet a lot she could not mention. In the end she penned a lively account of her motor trip through the gorge with its frequent slips and notices of 'falling debris'. She described the house, the old hotel and the green sheep-dotted hills of Glendene. Everyone here was very kind to her, she was enjoying herself immensely, so much so that she had decided to extend her visit maybe for as long as six months. There would be time enough later, she decided, to confide the real position here and her decision to forfeit her inheritance.

On the following day she was in the woolshed arranging cups and saucers on huge trays when Fred's call from the doorway alerted her. 'Here they come now!'

She hurried to join him at the opening and together they stood watching as a long line of cars, trucks and horse floats turned in at the main gate to park on the dried grass. She caught a glimpse of the huntsman's truck and still the procession advanced up the hill nearby.

It was a scene of activity with which she had once been familiar, but in vastly different circumstances, in another hemisphere, another life. There was, she mused, a wildness about this country, something free and untamed. She could imagine a man like Kevin Hawke revelling in wild gallops over the soaring hills, taking with ease the high barbed fences running across the slopes.

Unconsciously her gaze searched the scene where horses were being led from floats and guided down ramps of trucks and transporters. It wasn't, however, until riders and horses had assembled and were moving in the direction

of the woolshed that she caught sight of Kevin. His head
was turned aside and he was smiling into the face of a girl
riding alongside him. A girl with definite features, a firmly
moulded chin, black hair escaping from beneath the brim
of her hard hat and, it seemed to Christine, an air of
assurance. So this was Andrea. She watched the two riders
go by with a heaviness of spirit she couldn't understand.
Kevin hadn't even noticed her. He was much too taken up
with the conversation of the dark-haired girl at his side.
The next minute both riders had vanished over a rise.

At her side Fred was shading his eyes with his hand.
'Trust Andrea not to miss the opening hunt, even if she had
to come all the way back from Europe to be here in time
for it! She and Kevin, they've hunted together since they
were kids. She's taken a fall or two in her time, has
Andrea, but it never stopped her from turning up for the
next meet. She's got plenty of guts, that girl!'

Bully for her. Christine pulled herself up. What was happening to her? She simply couldn't understand herself, first
of all forgetting all about the break-up with Jason, something that two months previously she had imagined had
completely ruined her life. Now she was becoming worked
up merely because another girl hadn't allowed a mere hunting accident to leave her with all sorts of hang-ups about
the high jumps, even on these precipitous slopes. A girl
who Kevin Hawke was happy with, someone he had known
and liked for a long long time. Ridiculous the way his face
kept invading her mind. It wasn't as if she even liked him.
On the contrary, she had never felt so strongly about any
man!

It was early in the afternoon when a red-coated rider
appeared on the crest of a nearby hill to be followed by a
scattering of horses and riders.

Laurie, who had been peering through binoculars as he
stood at the lounge room windows, turned to Christine.
'They're on their way! How about bringing the big teapot
down to the shed?'

It wasn't long before dust-smeared riders were seeing to

their mounts, then strolling in the direction of the wool-shed.

Christine, making one of her trips between house and woolshed, tried not to look in the direction of Kevin and Andrea who were moving up the path together. Presently, however, she was too busy filling tea and coffee cups from massive containers to be able to notice anything else. Snatches of conversation drifted past her:

'He went like a dream, never even touched the wire! I didn't have to put on the brakes!'

'The footwork was tricky among the tree stumps.'

Then a voice she recognised. 'It was an older, solid sort of job with a bad take-off where the cattle had hollowed out the earth. Ginger got over okay, but he left me be-hind!' Christine's hand on the teapot stilled. The vet whom she had met yesterday. The next moment a thick-set young man came limping towards her.

'Gavin!' Her quick glance took in his pallor. 'Are you feeling all right?'

'Sure, sure. I had to bale out in a hurry, that's all. Col-lected a few bruises and my ankle doesn't feel quite the same. Nothing to complain of, though.' He leaned closer to murmur in her ear, 'Or that you couldn't fix.'

'Me?' She smiled up at him. 'What could I do?'

'Let me take you out somewhere next week.'

She finished pouring a cup of tea and a suntanned masculine hand took the cup from her. 'It's up to you.'

Christine, her attention taken up with her task, was about to answer when the crowd surged between them. 'More tea, please—coffee for me!' With a brief 'I'll keep in touch,' Gavin left her to attend to her duties.

Presently the riders who had been milling around her dispersed and she stole a glance towards Kevin and his female companion—she couldn't help herself. They stood together and appeared to be absorbed in their conversa-tion. Christine thought once again that Andrea, dark and forceful-looking, appeared to have plenty of assurance. Too much perhaps, for her loud tones and peals of laughter rose above the babel around her. Seen at close quarters the other girl's features were too strongly defined for beauty, but her frequent laughter and assured manner lent her an air of confidence that made up for imperfection of features. At least Kevin appeared to think so, judging by the attentive way in which he was inclining his head to catch Andrea's decisive tones.

At that moment she saw him leave Andrea's side and move to a position where he faced the gathering. Laughter and chatter died away and a hush fell over the groups as Kevin, speaking for the Master, summarised in fluent tones the day's activities. He went on to make mention of the Hunt's appreciation for Laurie having prepared the fences and thanked Ella for the mouthwatering spread she had provided in readiness for the return of the riders. Christine found she preferred gazing towards Kevin to listening to the conventional words. It was such a perfect opportunity to study him unobserved, and even knowing him as she did, she had to admit there was something about him, something that had to do with soft dark hair and firmly-cut lips.

The sombre green of his hunting jacket suited him, she thought. Exertion had lent colour to the tanned face and the dark hair falling over his forehead was damp with perspiration. Vaguely she became aware of his deep vibrant tones. '... not a right but a privilege. Good to know that things haven't changed at Glendene, not so far as the Hunt was concerned, even if old Ben was no longer there. It's our good fortune to be able to share in the continued hospitality of such a property as Glendene. Our thanks go to the new owner.'

As a thunder of applause broke out Christine thought with a shock of surprise: *He means me!* All eyes were on her, but she was aware only of Kevin, holding her glance with his deep compelling gaze. For a moment everything else fled her mind, then reality came flooding back. She was expected to say something in return!

She managed a tremulous smile, a low 'Thank you'. To

her relief no one appeared to expect more of her, for the talk and laughter had broken out once again. It didn't mean a thing to the crowd here today who was the owner of Glendene so long as old habits endured. Only one man here today cared deeply in the matter, and his opinions she could well do without.

At length the tea drew to a close and members of the club began to move down the high step to get into cars and trucks and continue their journey back to their own properties.

Kevin and Andrea were the last to leave. She knew because she was watching out of a corner of her eye. They paused beside Christine, who was stacking a pile of plates.

Smilingly she acknowledged the perfunctory thanks, all the time aware of Andrea's curious gaze. The other girl moved away, but Kevin paused beside her. 'I want to have a word with you.'

Her heart was behaving in an odd manner, leaping wildly, then settling again. So he had realised his unforgivable behaviour towards her and was anxious to make amends.

'A matter of business,' he added.

'Oh.' She avoided his gaze. 'I'm pretty busy at the moment.'

'How about my place, then? I'll call and pick you up tomorrow, right?' Before she could think of a suitable answer he had taken her silence for consent. 'See you then.'

As he joined Andrea, waiting at the entrance, she caught the forceful feminine tones. 'I thought you said she owned the whole outfit here. Does she *have* to work like that?'

Christine strained her ears to catch Kevin's deep tones. 'Apparently. She seems to enjoy it.'

'Oh well, I guess it takes all kinds.' The voices faded and Christine, moving to the doorway, watched the two climbing into Kevin's horse truck.

'You will keep that promise?' She was scarcely aware of Gavin's eager tones. 'You'll be doing something for the injured hurrying up the healing, think of it that way!'

'You don't look all that bad to me,' she smiled. 'But I'll come anyway.'

The way in which his pleasant young face lighted up at her words made up for a lot, she thought, though nothing could really make up for Kevin Hawke's cold accusing look across the table. And he wasn't even sorry!

CHAPTER SIX

CHRISTINE changed her garments three times before deciding on the outfit she would wear on her visit to Kevin's home. It wouldn't do for her to appear too dressed up as though this were an occasion, yet neither did she wish to appear too obviously country-style. In the end she settled for an ice-blue body shirt and well-worn jeans. She ran a comb through fine blonde hair, then touched her eyelids with shadow. An upward swirl of mascara on her lashes, pale pink lipstick, and she was ready. Her choice of clothing, like the make-up, she told herself, was for her own satisfaction. For hadn't Kevin gone out of his way to make it perfectly clear that any attraction she might have for other men simply left him cold? Nevertheless she knew she would feel more confident in her dealings with him were she to feel at ease with her appearance.

When she went into the kitchen she found Ella working at the big table. 'I'm going out for a bit,' Christine told her. 'Kevin Hawke is calling for me and taking me up to his house.'

'Kevin?' Ella looked surprised.

'Seems he wants to see me about something. A matter of business, he said.'

Ella's voice held a puzzled note. 'Funny he can't come over here and tell you about it.'

The same thought had crossed Christine's mind, but she

said lightly, 'Maybe Wendy wants to show me some of her work. She was telling me about the toys and slippers and things she makes from the fleeces.'

'And very attractive they are too.' Successfully diverted from the subject of that disturbing Kevin Hawke, Ella ran on, 'She sells her work to a local craft shop and makes quite a nice little income for herself. Not that she can't do with the money, seeing her parents left her quite unprovided for. She hasn't had much fun in her life ... all that time she spent in hospital when she was younger. The only love affair she ever had, if you could call it a love affair, was with a young student doctor she got friendly with a couple of years ago. He was a studious, shy sort of man with untidy black hair and a quite fierce expression. Wendy used to talk about him a lot at that time, but he went overseas to Edinburgh to study and I think that was the end of the romance. She never mentions him now. Of course she wouldn't, the way things are with her and Kevin——' Ella broke off with a significant glance towards Christine.

'How do you mean?'

'Oh, nothing, only Kevin has something of a reputation around these parts for keeping friendly with a girl for ever so long, but somehow he never gets around to marriage.'

'You mean, like Andrea?'

'That's right ... and Wendy. Mind you, he just may be waiting for her twenty-first birthday party to make the big announcement.'

'Maybe he doesn't want to marry every girl he happens to be friendly with, even if she does happen to have wedding bells in mind.' Why was she going to all this trouble to defend Kevin of all men?

Ella was silent for a moment. 'There's no denying,' she murmured, 'that he's mighty attractive. All the same——'

'But, Ella,' teased Christine, 'didn't you tell me that Uncle Ben had a lot of time for Kevin Hawke? That in his book there was no one like him?'

'So I did, and I'm much of the same opinion myself, but

then,' Ella's glance moved to Christine's glowing young face, 'it's not quite the same thing. I don't happen to be young *and* as pretty as a picture!'

Christine burst into laughter. 'Ella! If you're worrying about Kevin Hawke and me, you can forget it. I can take care of myself! Honestly!'

Famous last words. The dark goblin deep in her mind sprang to life, but Christine pushed it aside and tried to concentrate on Ella's tones.

'Don't say I didn't warn you! Although,' she added slowly, taking in Christine's pale satiny complexion and great brown eyes, the air of exquisite perfection that seemed to be a part of this girl from England, 'who knows, the boot might be on the other foot one of these days!'

In view of Kevin's feelings towards her, feelings he made no attempt to conceal, Christine considered the possibility to be extremely unlikely. The next moment her gaze went to the window and she caught sight of a long red car that was nosing in at the entrance. 'Here he comes now!' She swung the strap of her leather shoulder bag over her shoulder and went out to meet him.

Slamming the car door shut, Kevin turned and came striding down the path towards her. He wore the same working gear as did Laurie and the other young men of the district working on the land. Bright cotton shirt, narrow drill trousers, a low chased leather belt, narrow boots. Yet something about him set him apart. Could it be, she wondered, the way he walked as if he were master of his world? And why not? Didn't he own a vast hill country sheep station, and in this corner of the world that counted for quite a lot. Suddenly, despite the unhappy experience he had put her through at their last meeting, she was feeling extraordinarily, inexplicably lighthearted. She tried not to look as happy as she was feeling and forced her voice to a casual note. 'You're making an early start today?'

'Not too early for you. All ready and waiting for me?'

'I saw your car coming up the drive.'

'Come on then, let's go!'

They swung out of the drive and headed down the hill. Before long they were skirting great plantations of ripening corn and vineyards with their crimson and green vines. Then they were turning into a lonely metal road winding upwards among cleared hills. The only signs of civilisation, so far as Christine could discern, were an occasional farmhouse with its long boundary fences of tall poplars and vast, sheep-dotted paddocks.

Kevin swung around a sharp bend, then braked to a sudden stop just in time to avoid colliding with a black steer ambling nonchalantly across the roadway. Other steers, grazing in the long grass at the edge of the road, followed. As they waited for the stragglers to pass, Christine asked curiously, 'Are they yours?'

He shook his dark head. 'Not guilty. Wandering stock is always a bit of a hazard on quiet roads around here.'

'I suppose so.' It was difficult, she reflected, to make light conversation with a man who had gone to such pains to humiliate one, and yet ... could it be that today's invitation was a gesture of repentance on his part? For a moment her heart lifted, then a quick sideways glance towards the strong masculine profile at her side made the thought seem ridiculous. He wouldn't be one for regrets and apologies, not 'the King', and especially where she herself was concerned. Gathering her defences together, she said crisply, 'What was it that you wanted to see me about?'

His gaze was fixed on the last steer meandering in front of the car. 'Tell you all about it when we get there!' He put a hand to the starter and they sped forward. 'I guess this is all new territory to you?' The warmth of his unexpected smile sent her thoughts spinning in wild confusion.

'Oh, it is! I——' The eager words came to a halt. No doubt he was attempting to soften her up for purposes of his own.

Apparently he did not notice her lack of response. 'Mata-Rangi isn't far now. You'll get your first sight of it in a minute.' They swung around a hairpin bend and Christine looked up towards the gracious old homestead set on a spur of the hill. Sheltered by tall poplars turning to gold and crimson tints, surrounded by sweeping lawns and flowering shrubs, the two-storied house with its gables and wide verandahs lay dreaming in the sunshine. To Christine, coming on the scene so suddenly, the homestead high in the lonely hills had a quality of unreality. 'It's so beautiful,' she breathed, scarcely realising she was giving voice to her thoughts.

He had braked to a stop and, eyes narrowed, was following her gaze. 'I thought it would get you.' His voice had a deep soft timbre she had never heard before. Just for once, she thought, he seemed to have forgotten the identity of his passenger. 'This is the way to see Mata-Rangi for the first time, at this point of the road, on this sort of a day.' His gaze lifted to the translucent blue. 'Still, sky without a cloud, blue smoke rising back in the hills where the boys are burning off scrub and fern.'

Christine could scarcely believe her ears. This softer side of his nature came as a surprise to her—but then, she reminded herself, he was enthusing about his land, his home. Aloud she asked curiously, 'Mata-Rangi ... what does it mean?'

He grinned. 'You could have worked that one out for yourself! The Maoris had a pretty lyrical way with them when it came to place names, and this time they really hit the spot. It happens to be "Fringe of Heaven".'

'Oh!'

'Would you believe? It's a hundred years old and yet the place has never been finished according to the original plan. It's true.' Something in his eye was disturbing, definitely. 'Blame an old Maori prophecy that was made at the time Mata-Rangi was being built.'

'A—prophecy?' She was having difficulty in meeting his alive, penetrating glance.

'That's right. It was said at the time by the Maori *tohunga* that the house would never be finished until a descendant of the original family married a girl who had come to this land from over the sea. My father took a bride from the next station. Me,' the strongly marked brows rose quizzically, 'the question doesn't arise—yet.'

'Well,' she said gaily, 'that lets me out!' The moment the words had left her lips she was appalled at what she had said. She couldn't imagine what had impelled her to say such a thing, and to him of all men! Put it down to the nervous antagonism he seemed to arouse in her. Wildly she rushed into speech with the first thing that came into her head. 'I mean, I arrived here by air! A wonderful air trip it was too!' she heard herself rattling on, in a frantic effort to change the subject. 'It was the plane with the Maori design on the wing.'

'You mean the *koro*, the mark of the questing islanders who first came to this country in their hand-hewn canoes?'

'Yes, yes!' Bless those wandering seafarers, she breathed silently. Bless anything that rescued her from the implications of a dangerous subject.

The next moment, catching the amused glint in Kevin's eyes, she wasn't quite so sure about the rescue.

'Actually,' he was saying, 'the plans for the room that was never built originally have been drawn up on three different occasions through the years, but each time there was a hitch of some sort and the idea was shelved. Not that it mattered as things turned out.'

She glanced towards him uncertainly. 'Why, what was it meant to be originally?'

Again the amused glint in his eyes and something else, something she couldn't sustain. 'Tell you some time.'

'Oh!' She didn't know what to say. Surely he couldn't take the old Maori prophecy seriously? Yet apparently he did. She would never understand him, never. Aloud she queried, 'All those cleared hills at the back of the homestead? I suppose they're all part of Mata-Rangi?' She pronounced the soft Maori syllables carefully.

'That's right,' his tone was careless.

'It must take an awful lot of staff to run it. How many men have you working on the place?'

'Just the usual for a station around here. Shepherds, mechanic, odd job man, gardener—and Bob.' Kevin grinned. 'He's the most important one of the bunch.'

'You mean he's in charge of the stock and everything?'

'You could put it that way. He's the guy who keeps the books, sees to the accounts, all that stuff.' He pressed the accelerator. 'We'd better get cracking. Wendy's waiting at home and she'll be thinking we're never going to turn up. She's taken quite a fancy to you.'

Wendy. Christine felt a stab go through her. Jealousy? There was no other word for it. What did Wendy *really* mean to Kevin? He spoke the name as if making mention of a relative or family friend, and yet ... and why should it matter to her? The answer came with staggering impact. *Because you're falling in love with him*, with HIM, a man who has for you nothing but contempt! Shaken by the revelation of her feelings, she stared blindly out of the window. They were dropping down into the filtered shade of a gully where thickly-growing native trees crowded the track and the air was cool and fragrant with the damp earthy smell of the bush. Presently they swept out into full sunlight to rattle over a cattlestop and take a track winding towards the homestead above. They were passing two modern bungalows with their clipped green lawns when Christine, trying to focus her thoughts on anything but the man beside her, asked curiously, 'Who lives in those houses?'

'The two married shepherds and their families.'

They sped past clusters of farm buildings, stables, garages and the mellow red timbers of a woolshed, then he drew to a stop outside wide entrance gates. He swung around, grinning, 'The passenger's job!'

Christine sat still, staring blankly back at him. If he imagined she was going to leap out of the car to open gates for him he was mighty mistaken!

'But I'll let you off this time.' Leaving the motor idling, he got out to swing open the gates and closed them behind the car.

Presently they were sweeping up a long driveway between green lawns with their blaze of flower borders, to pull up on the wide driveway of the homestead.

They were mounting the steps together when Wendy appeared on the sunny verandah above. 'Hello, Christine! Come in! I thought you were never going to get here to see us!'

Something about the words sent a chill through her, then she told herself not to be so stupidly imaginative. What if Wendy did speak as if she were mistress here, or about to be? It could mean nothing at all. She pushed the niggling thoughts aside. She was only half aware of Wendy's excited chatter as she and Kevin went along a carpeted hall, matching their steps to the girl's slow limping gait.

At the door of the lounge room they were met by Kevin's mother, a slim tanned woman with beautifully arranged silver hair. Introductions over, Christine dropped down on a low lounge seat close to the open french windows with their view of distant hills. A swift glance around the walls of the room revealed photographs of Kevin with his prize-winning show-jumpers. Ribbons and trophies were displayed in glass cases and there were pictures of horse trials, and events held in various parts of the country as well as in Japan and Australia, in which Kevin had taken a leading part.

Before long he was called away to see to an urgent matter outside, and Christine found that Mrs Hawke was very easy to talk to. The older woman had travelled extensively. She had made trips to England and now plied Christine with eager questions regarding the great London stores with their incredible and eye-catching displays of every possible commodity ranging from foreign foodstuffs to high fashion garments. Christine gathered that Marie Hawke's interests ran to social life, entertaining and golf, rather than to riding or the weaving and spinning that occupied the leisure time of so many of the wives of local farmers.

Christine smiled and chatted, but all the time her thoughts were occupied with a question she couldn't seem to banish from her mind. What was it that Kevin wanted of her today?

All at once she realised Mrs Hawke had followed her gaze towards a framed portrait hanging on the wall opposite. The dark bearded face, Christine thought, bore a surprising resemblance to Kevin.

The older woman seemed to radar in on her musing. 'Looks a lot like Kevin, doesn't he? That's his grandfather. He was one of a large family and so was my husband.' A shadow passed over her face. 'There was a time once when I thought—hoped I was going to follow the Hawke family pattern, but after Kevin came along I lost the baby who was to be his playmate and the doctors told me I could never have another child.' Her gaze went to Wendy who, with a mention of making afternoon tea, had moved towards the door. 'I guess,' she said on a sigh, 'that having Wendy around the place is about the nearest I'll ever get to having a daughter of my own!'

Once again Christine was conscious of a prick of jealousy. She wrenched her mind back to the friendly tones. 'Now,' Mrs Hawke smiled her charming smile, 'it's over to Kevin, and goodness knows when that will be! I simply can't get rid of the man!' Beneath the laughing words Christine caught a ring of pride. 'Once he gets married,' she threw out her hands in a gesture of despair, 'if *ever*, Dad and I will get a smaller place built on the property and move into that, or maybe we'll take a flat in town.' Christine followed her gaze through open french doors to Kevin who was striding along the path below. Mrs Hawke sighed. 'He looks so self-sufficient, doesn't he? As if he'd never need anyone. He doesn't look as if he'd get married, somehow.'

'Maybe,' Christine couldn't resist saying, 'he's been spoiled by women?'

'Could be, but then again you never can tell with men, even one's own son! Trouble is they never *tell* you anything, anything that matters romance-wise, that is. Though lately,' she added thoughtfully, 'I've wondered if——'

She broke off as Wendy came into the room, pushing a tea-waggon loaded with a fluffy sponge cake, cream-filled, and heated bread and pastry shells filled with savoury spreads.

'Perhaps,' Christine said lightly, 'you treat him too well at home.' If only Kevin's mother had finished what she had been about to say!

Her husband, coming into the room at that moment, went to stand beside Wendy. 'You've been baking again, lass? I thought this visit was supposed to be a holiday?'

Wendy's thin face flushed with pleasure. 'I *like* doing it. Anyway, I was only helping Mum!'

Christine was only half aware of the older man's greeting. Mum! Was that what Marie Hawke had meant when she had spoken of the nearest thing to a daughter? A daughter-in-law? With an effort she brought her mind back to the thick-set man of middle age with his weathered brown face thick greying hair and cheerful smile. 'You'll have to excuse my working gear, miss,' he was saying, indicating heavy work boots, cotton shirt and well worn slacks, 'I've been out on the run shifting some steers—thanks, love,' he took a cup of tea from Wendy, balancing the fragile china with work-roughened hands. To Christine he appeared so essentially a man of the land that she found herself speculating on how such a man would adjust to life in a city apartment. But of course, she reminded herself, he and Marie might retire to a smaller house here, and in any case they wouldn't be living far from Mata-Rangi, only a few miles. He could always spend time on the station with Kevin and his wife. *His wife.* There she went again, delving into matters that were none of her concern, thinking of HIM. Somehow she must make herself remember that Kevin Hawke's love life had nothing to do with her ... unfortunately.

Teacups were all but emptied when Kevin returned to the room to down a quick drink and eye Christine with the intent gaze she found it so difficult to meet. 'Sorry, folks, but I'll have to borrow Christine for a while. I'd like to show her around a bit outside.'

. His mother rose to her feet. 'Run along, then, both of you.'

'Don't be too long away,' Wendy cried eagerly, 'I want Christine to tell me what she thinks of my work.'

Because she was very curious about the reason for Kevin having invited her to his home Christine got up and together they moved down the long flight of steps and out into the driveway. Soon they were taking a path up a slope where mares and foals grazed in wide paddocks. She hurried along beside him trying to match his long steps. 'If it's horses you wanted to see me about I'm not very knowledgeable,' she lied. The next minute the interest in her eyes belied the words as a grey hunter trotted towards the railings. 'Isn't he just a picture!' she exclaimed.

'That's Bluey!'

They paused together leaning on the sliprails and she caressed the velvety muzzle of the big grey horse that she recognised as the mount Kevin had ridden at the recent hunt. Forgetting her pose of disinterest, she said with enthusiasm, 'We've got a big grey at Glendene too!'

'You're telling me! I know all about your uncle's Trooper, that's why I happen to be in the market for him. I put it to Laurie first, I had an idea he might want to take him over from you, but he told me as far as he was concerned the deal was on but it was over to you.' She realised he was regarding her steadily. 'He's something special and I'd very much like to have him—at your own price, of course, if he's available.'

The ball, she realised, was in her court and she took full advantage of it. 'He's not for sale,' she told him.

He looked taken aback. 'Why not?'

'Just,' she fumbled for words, 'I want to keep him, that's all.'

'You?' He eyed her sceptically. 'But you don't ride, you told me——'

'I might ... one of these days. I took Brownie out over the hills the other day.'

'It's scarcely the same thing,' he returned dryly. 'Trooper's known to have a devil of a hard mouth. Believe me, it takes a strong man to hold him in check——'

'Like you?' she taunted.

He ignored the jibe. 'That's right, or your uncle. Old Ben always said that Trooper was the pick of all the hunters he'd bred and trained himself over the years.'

'Oh, really?' Christine feigned indifference and he glanced towards her sharply. 'I thought you had a mount already?' Careful, Christine girl, you're not supposed to know about hunts and horses. 'At least,' she went on in a rush of words, 'Bluey looked big and strong when he went past the house on the way to the hunt the other day.'

'He's terrific, but up here in the hills we hunt two or three times a week, and believe me, the steep slopes around here aren't easy on horses, even ones as tough and willing as Bluey here and your Trooper. You need to have quite a few mounts in reserve and change them around if you're not going to tire them out before the end of the season.'

She said slowly, 'And that was what you wanted to see me about? Business, you said?'

'What else?' His mocking grin lighted up the dark face. 'It would have to be, wouldn't it, to get you to come over to my place?'

Her heart began to thud ridiculously and it was with an effort she made her voice cool and steady. 'You mean——'

'I mean,' he said very low, 'that I want to do a deal with you, Christine.' The thought came from nowhere that on his lips her name seemed to ring like silver bells, or were the bells ringing in her heart? A sudden wild excitement was taking over and his voice seemed to be coming from a distance. 'How about letting me have your uncle's hunter?'

'Let you have him?' she heard her own voice echo stupidly. Somehow she managed to pull herself together. 'No, no, I'm sorry.' She drew a deep breath and looked directly ahead, for something told her it would be easier to do battle away from the distraction of those disturbing eyes. 'I don't want to sell.' A sudden thought struck her and she glanced towards him, wide-eyed. 'Unless—did my uncle promise you——'

'Good grief, no! He had no idea that for him time was running out.'

'I see.'

'So it's over to you!' Unexpectedly his tone softened. 'Why not, Christine?' He was standing very close, but he wasn't even touching her, so why did she feel this strange emotion taking hold of her so that all at once it was difficult to make herself remember things like evening the score with him and saying no, no, no. If only the nearness of him didn't affect her like this!

'If it's the money,' he was saying, 'you don't have to worry. I don't bargain for what I want. I'll give you the top price going for a first class hunter. You can check with Laurie if you're not happy about it.'

'Oh no, it's not the price,' she said.

'What then?' There was a note of genuine puzzlement in his deep tones. 'Trooper's a great horse, but at the moment he's badly in need of exercise, work.'

Christine had a sensation of fighting her way up from deep waters. She said very low, 'Laurie will take him out.'

'So could I! If it's time you want, you can think over the offer at the weekend and let me know.'

'You do want him badly, don't you?' It was a mistake, she realised the next minute, to look up at him. She saw a light leap into his eyes.

'Christine, do me a favour, will you? Your uncle would have been all for it.'

His hand reached out to cover hers, his fingers warm on the pulse of her wrist, and once again bells were ringing all over the place. Still in a state of bemusement, she heard herself say, 'You can have him.'

'I can?' Elation threaded his tone. 'Tremendous! It's a lucky day for any man when he comes across a hunter of

Trooper's calibre. It only happens once or twice in a life-time, I'd say. I'll make you out a cheque for a couple of thousand bucks—okay with you?'

Evidently he misconstrued her silence. 'I doubt if you'll get a better offer in the country, and there's no need for you to concern yourself over Trooper. Believe me, I'll take good care of him. I'll exercise him myself. There's a resident smithy on the place and the vet is always around here for one thing or another. He's new in the district, but he seems to know his job——' He broke off, eyeing her with a veiled glance. 'What am I saying? You know all about the vet. I saw him hanging around you at the Hunt breakfast the other day.'

Hanging around! Was there anything concerning herself of which he failed to take notice? It just went to show how deep were his feelings towards her, feelings of dislike and re-sentment. One more victim caught in the web she wove for masculine admirers, was that the direction in which his thoughts were running? Anger rose in her and with it a stab of pain. 'Gavin? Yes, I know him.' An impulse she couldn't define prompted her to add, 'He's taking me out to dinner one night soon.'

'Lucky Gavin!'

As they turned and began to stroll back to the house her thoughts were racing in wild confusion. It was ridiculous, it was against all logic that she should have given in to Kevin and sold him Trooper, yet that was precisely what she had done. It had taken just one word, his softly-spoken 'Chris-tine' in that low caressing tone, and every sensible thought had fled her mind. She tried to console herself with the argument that it was a matter of business. She had ob-tained a fair price for the hunter, hadn't she? She wouldn't be staying here indefinitely, she felt a wrench at the thought, and chances were that she wouldn't get her nerve back sufficiently to ride the hard-mouthed horse, so of course to sell him was the only sensible course. But in her heart she knew that no amount of rationalising could alter the fact that she had weakly given in to Kevin Hawke. And all the time he despised her.

When they reached the house he said offhandedly, 'If I know Wendy she'll keep you busy for the next half hour. I'll come in with you and run you home when you're through with her.'

His words struck a chill in her heart. Just like that. Clearly now that he had achieved his objective in bringing her here he was as cool and distant as ever. Nothing was any different, not really.

Back in the lounge room once more they were greeted by a smiling Wendy.

'You've been busy,' Kevin grinned, and Christine followed his gaze towards the articles fashioned from fluffy sheepskins that were displayed on seats, chairs and low tables. The fleeces, dyed to glowing jewel shadings of crimson and violet, pink and orange, had been made into moccasins, soft toys for young children, purses and mats.

'I'm taking these to the shop soon,' Wendy told Christine, 'but I wanted you to see them first. Do you like the car seat covers?' She indicated the natural wool fleeces, then smiled towards Kevin. 'I'm making covers for your car seats, what colour would you like?'

He was smoking as he strolled idly around the room inspecting the girl's handiwork. 'What's wrong with the original?' he said with a grin. 'That'll do me!'

'Whatever you say, Kevin. I've measured up your car seats, so I know they'll fit.'

Mrs Hawke made a goodnatured grimace. 'There goes my one idea for a Christmas gift for him!' She appealed to Christine, 'Don't you agree men are difficult when it comes to giving them presents? One never knows what to give them. Especially,' she sent a significant glance towards her son, 'when it comes to a man who has everything in the world he could possibly want.'

'Not quite everything, not by a long way!' Kevin was looking towards *her*, Christine realised with a sense of shock. What could he mean by that? Could he be referring to a special girl-friend, a wife? A girl who, unlike the general run of women he knew, failed to respond to his undoubted charisma and dark good looks. *A girl like herself?*

'These are for you, Christine!'

She became aware that Wendy was holding out a pair of sheepskin slippers, great furry balls of pale pink fleece.

'For me? Oh, thank you!' Christine hesitated, afraid of giving offence. 'But you must let me pay for them.'

'Oh no, *please*, they're a present!' It was, Christine thought, the voice of a hurt child. 'I made them specially.'

'And I love them!' Because she felt it would give Wendy pleasure to see her work appreciated, Christine said gaily, 'I always think that a gift should be used!' Kicking off her rubber jandals, she slipped bare feet into the gigantic fun slippers.

'I knew you'd like them!' The grey eyes seemed larger than ever in the thin face. 'If you like I'll make some slippers for you to send back to your friends in England. Just tell me the colours you'd like,' Wendy offered eagerly, 'and I'll make them. Only I won't let you pay for them!' She was so anxious to please, Christine realised, her one thought was to give, give, give.

'I'll let you know,' Christine temporised, not wishing to take advantage of the generous offer.

It was no use. Wendy ignored the words. 'I'll get started on them right away. I've got plenty of orange-coloured fleece here with me.'

Mrs Hawke said smilingly, 'It looks as though you'll be settling down to work while you're here, Wendy—excuse me for just a minute,' she was moving towards the door.

'I'll try!' Wendy called after her. The girl's face was radiant with suppressed excitement. 'Though how anyone can expect me to settle to anything when——'

'I got the idea,' Kevin's deep tones cut across the emotional outburst, 'that all that was to be our secret until next month?'

'Oh, it is! It is! It just goes to show,' she ran on in her

guileless way, 'how you can get carried away with happiness and forget all about secrets. Anyway, it won't be for long. I know you're right about it, Kevin. It will be so much more fun to tell everyone on the night of my twenty-first! Only a few weeks away now!'

Christine sat motionless, swept by a sick feeling of anguish. So it was true, what everyone in the district had suspected? The truth that in her mind she had somehow contrived to ignore. Because it was too painful to face? Once again she heard Ella's confidential tones. 'I wouldn't be surprised if they didn't announce their engagement on that night, Kevin and Wendy. A good thing in a way it would be too, to link up two well-known local families. The only trouble is Wendy is so frail she doesn't look strong enough ever to have any family, but she might surprise us all yet.' So that was what he wanted, a child-wife, someone who hung on his every word and deferred to him in every possible way. A girl who would never ever cross him, never cause the blue eyes to be cold and implacable the way they so often were when he was with her. Oblivious of Wendy's excited chatter, at last she came to terms with herself. I've loved him from the moment I met him, she thought, only I didn't realise that love could masquerade as hate and it doesn't matter anyway. *If only he doesn't guess, if only I can keep my feelings to myself, pretend, pretend.*

'You're coming to my party, you know,' the gay childish voice penetrated the fog of misery, 'you've got to! Don't forget you're a Kiwi now, one of us!'

'We're holding the celebration here,' Marie Hawke had returned to the room, 'seeing that Wendy's aunt isn't fit enough to put on anything like that in town. Anyway, why not here? Mata-Rangi is home to Wendy and the old ballroom will be ideal for a party.' Her smiling gaze went to Christine. 'You'll be getting an invitation in the post.'

'It's kind of you to ask me, but,' Christine grasped at the first excuse that came to mind, for how could she bear to attend the gathering, watching Wendy and Kevin announce their wedding plans, 'I'm afraid I might not be there by then. I might have to return to England.'

Wendy's face fell. 'But you can't go until after the party! Please say you'll stay that long,' she pleaded.

'I'll try.' Could that be her own voice sounding much the same as usual, just as if there were no hollow feeling in the pit of her stomach? For how could she refuse Wendy's plea? Close on the thought came another. No matter what it costs me somehow I'll stick it out and stay until the lawyer's confirmation comes through telling me that the gift of the property has gone through and Laurie is the legal owner of Glendene. I want to stay long enough to be able to see Kevin's face when he learns the truth. Tears sparkled in her eyes and she blinked them determinedly away. So that he'll think of me ... differently. An icy wind seemed to sweep over her spirit. If he ever thinks of me at all.

Perhaps, however, she wasn't as skilful at hiding her feelings as she had imagined, for Wendy's anxious glance sought her averted face. 'Don't you care for parties, Christine?'

'Of course I do!'

Wendy looked unconvinced. 'There'll be dancing, you know. Just because I don't dance, this stupid leg of mine, it doesn't mean I don't want everyone else to enjoy themselves. You'll have a good time!'

A good time. Christine wrenched her mind back to the eager tones. 'It will be such fun, having all our friends here together. You see, I've lived around here all my life, except for the two years I went to stay in Auckland to study for my Diploma of Fine Arts——'

'And got it,' Kevin put in warmly, 'don't leave out the most important part!'

'Thanks to you,' Wendy returned laughingly.

'I don't know how you make that out!'

'I do, and so do you, only you won't admit it!' The girl's animated gaze went to Christine. 'It's all due to him, any success I've had! Honestly, I never would have got up the courage to leave here and stay in a hostel in the city. I

would have turned the idea down flat or put it off for ever,
I know I would, but Kevin just wouldn't let me. He kept
telling me I had some talent in painting and practically
forced me to enrol for the course, then he wrote me every
week to make sure I was working, or maybe it was so I
wouldn't be too homesick for the country.' The light tones
rose excitedly. 'And when I did get my diploma he was so
thrilled, anyone would think he'd done it all himself! So he
did in a way——'

Kevin was looking increasingly embarrassed. 'Cut it out,'
he muttered gruffly. 'What did I do? Nothing, except believe you had it in you.'

'But don't you see,' Wendy's voice was tremulous with
emotion, 'that was everything!' She appealed to Christine,
'You'll have to forgive me for going on about him and what
he did for me. Not,' she added laughingly, 'that I'll ever be
a celebrity with my paintings, but I've sold a few and I get
a lot of pleasure out of it, even though it's my sheepskin
work that gives me a living. Kevin would never admit it,
but I knew I wouldn't have got the contracts to sell my
work in the shops in towns all over the country if he hadn't
gone to all the trouble to arrange it for me.'

'Hell, it's you who has to do the work!' Kevin was looking uncomfortable. 'Come off it, Wendy! Christine will be
getting browned off with all this.'

'I guess it's only natural.' Christine got to her feet. 'It's
time I was getting back, I'm afraid.'

She caught a light of relief that leaped into Kevin's eyes.
Was he anxious to be rid of her now that he had got what
he wanted? Or could it be, she wondered wryly, that even
the master of Mata-Rangi could tire of a session of un-
adulterated hero-worship from the lips of the girl he
planned to marry?

On the drive back to Glendene Kevin said little and
Christine, lost in her thoughts, made no effort at conversation. A numbness was creeping through her body,
a heaviness of spirit, and all the time the betraying tears
gathered at the back of her eyelids. She blinked them away.

Wouldn't you think, she mused wistfully, that knowing what she did, she wouldn't *let* herself care for him so deeply, so hopelessly? It was no use; every tiny thing about him was precious to her. She stole a sideways glance in his direction, achingly conscious of the tanned well-shaped hand on the steering wheel, the way the thick dark hair clustered at the nape of his neck. *I love you*, Kevin, but you'll never know! She wrenched her glance aside and stared dully out of the open window. Everything was the same as when they had passed this way earlier in the day, the clear warm sunshine, the vista of bush-filled gully and encircling hills, yet nothing was the same for her—not now.

They were nearing their destination when Kevin shot her one of those penetrating glances. 'You're very quiet, Christine. Not regretting our deal, are you?'

'Deal?' Her eyes were bright with unshed tears. 'Oh, you mean about Trooper? No, of course not.'

He let the subject drop and a few minutes later they swept into the entrance of Glendene and up the yard. A grey van was parked by the fence and from the back of the vehicle various dogs of different breeds and sizes eyed the car as it swept past.

Kevin flicked her a meaningful glance. 'Got trouble at your place?'

Christine fell into the trap. 'Not that I know of.' The next moment she braced herself mentally for one of his abrasive comments concerning the real reason for the vet's visit. She knew by the derisive look in his eyes what he was thinking. To her surprise, however, he made no further comment and presently he saw her to the door. 'I can pick up Trooper tomorrow, then? Okay with you, Christine?'

She nodded carelessly. 'Any time.' What did it matter, what did anything matter now?

'See you then.' He sketched a brief salute in the air, turned and left her.

In the house she found Gavin waiting for her, his open pleasant face lighting up as she entered the kitchen.

'Hi!' She tossed her shoulder bag on a chair and tried to look as though she hadn't learned something today that had shattered her world. 'No one else about? I thought Ella or Fred would be here?'

He grinned. 'It wasn't Ella or Fred I came to see.'

She forced a smile. 'Have you been here long?'

'Only five minutes.' He eyed her laughingly. 'It was so lucky! I happened to get a call out this way. It didn't take me long to fix the pony, so of course I couldn't resist stopping the van here, not when it was on my way back to town.'

'According to Ella,' Christine roused herself to say teasingly, 'you seem to have an awful lot of ailing animals to see to along this road. What's wrong with them all?' she enquired innocently, 'some sort of epidemic?'

'Just chance,' he protested, his twinkling eyes giving the lie to his words. 'Put it down to luck, like my landing the job down this way just at the right time. You wouldn't like to offer me coffee, by any chance? I skipped breakfast this morning and the pangs of hunger are starting.'

'Serves you right,' but she filled the big chrome jug and plugged the lead into the socket. 'You men who go flatting on your own never look after yourselves properly. The awful hours you work, I should think what you need is a——'

'A wife?' Suddenly his tone was serious. 'What would you say to that, Christine?'

Avoiding the implication, she said hastily, 'I was going to say that what you need is a housekeeper,' and reached up to a shelf above her head for coffee mugs.

'I've got a better idea. Why not come out with me to a restaurant tomorrow night? You're always promising to let me take you out, but you never make a date. You said yourself that I needed building up——'

'I said you needed——' She broke off in some confusion. No need to go into that again. 'If you like.'

She stared blindly down at the coffee mugs. Why not go out with him? She felt comfortable and at ease with Gavin,

The warmth of his feelings for her seemed to melt a little of the frozen core deep inside that had come when she had first known about—*Don't think of Kevin. He's nothing to you. A stranger who chanced to cross your path for a brief time. Put him out of your mind. If only I could!*

'Hey, steady on!' Gavin's warning voice jerked her back to the present. 'You're spilling boiling water all over the place!'

'Help!' She stared dazedly down at the pool of water spreading over the table. 'I don't know what I was thinking of!'

Goodnaturedly he picked up a rubber sponge mop from the sink bench and began wiping up the liquid. 'So long as it wasn't Kevin!'

'Kevin?' The light that leaped in her eyes would have betrayed her, but Gavin was busy with his task and did not notice. She said thickly, 'What ... makes you say that?'

'Joke, Christine, joke! Just that I happened to hear on the grapevine that you were at his place today.'

She let out her breath on a sigh of relief. 'That's right, he wanted to see me about buying Trooper, Uncle Ben's hunter, you know?'

'I know Trooper. Did you get a good price for him?'

'Two thousand dollars—is that all right?'

He whistled under his breath. 'I'll say it's all right! It happens to be top price and then some! Know something, Christine,' the young bearded face regarded her laughingly, 'you're a darn good business woman!'

She said with a shaky smile, 'Not really. I just left it to him to name a price. It was a bit risky, I suppose——'

'Not with Kevin!'

'I know what you mean.' Absently she stirred her coffee. Somehow, in spite of all their differences, she did trust Kevin to be fair. She would never doubt his integrity, it was only on personal grounds, she reflected wistfully, that he let her down. She pulled her thoughts together—there she went again, letting herself dwell endlessly on HIM! She wrenched her mind aside and in an effort to change the subject, said quickly, 'There was a girl staying there, Wendy her name was. She makes toys and mats and all sorts of things from sheepskin and sells them locally.' She was speaking jerkily. 'They seem very good to her, Kevin and his mother and father. Wendy has sold some of her paintings too, she seems to be quite an artist.'

'Is she now?' He seemed little interested in the subject of the other girl. 'Can't say I know her, but her name rings a bell. That's right! It was when I was out at Mata-Rangi last week. They had a spot of bother with one of the station hacks and the old man said something about their putting on a do at the house for Wendy's twenty-first. I gathered I could expect an invitation in the mail.'

For something to say she asked, 'Going to accept it?'

'Depends.' His laughing face sobered. 'If I can take you with me I'll be there.'

'Why not?' Beneath the light words her thoughts milled in confusion. Somehow she had to get through the night of Wendy's party, and at least having Gavin with her would lighten the painful ordeal of being forced to listen to that special announcement. She became aware of his elated tones.

'That's mighty! You get to town and buy yourself a new dress to celebrate and I'll keep my fingers crossed that no urgent calls come through to take me out that night.'

A new dress to celebrate?

His kindly gaze rested on her downcast face. 'What's wrong, Christine? Can't you afford a new dress, is that it? Not to worry. Hasn't any guy ever told you that a girl who looks like you do doesn't need a new dress to bowl 'em over!' The teasing accents were suddenly serious. 'I mean it.' He reached out a hand and she felt his warm clasp on her bare arm. 'Every guy at the party will think the same, but that's my problem.'

'Don't be absurd!' At the sharpness of her tone he glanced at her in surprise.

'Sorry,' she said in a muffled voice, 'I'm a bit on edge today.' She gave an unsteady laugh. 'I'd better snap out of it before you give me a shot for distemper or something!'

He said softly, 'What's the trouble, Christine? You can tell me, you know. Something worrying you?'

'No, no, of course not!' She put on her most winning smile and was relieved when Ella entering the room at that moment put an end to the conversation. Shortly afterwards Gavin left and went out to his van.

Christine couldn't seem to think straight today, not since she had learned of that impending announcement Wendy was waiting to make public. No use denying the truth. Kevin filled her mind, her heart; she could concentrate on nothing else, not even now when she had learned that he was planning to marry another girl.

All the time one part of her mind was busily engaged in chatting with Ella. What did Christine think, Ella wanted to know, she should prepare for dinner tonight?

'Lamb chops!' It was the first thought that came into her head. On another level, however, her thoughts were churning wildly. She didn't have to stay and witness the happiness of the other two at the coming celebration. She could just slip away from here for ever. It was only a matter of a telephone call to arrange an air booking back to London. But all the time she knew she couldn't wrench away from the sight of Kevin herself. Just seeing him, hearing the tones of his voice, was sufficient to keep her here. That was how deeply in love with him she was, even though she knew all the time that it was hopeless, hopeless.

The thoughts whirled endlessly through her distraught mind. She had to stay for another reason. For come what may she refused to allow fate to cheat her of the moment when, the property gift legally finalised, she could tell Kevin that Glendene no longer belonged to her, that she had delayed her departure all these months until she was certain everything was in order and Laurie had become the man in possession. Just so that Kevin would *know*, just so maybe he would think kindly of her now and again. It wasn't much, she thought on a long sigh, just one moment in time when she could tell him the truth, watch his expression change, but it was all she had to look forward to and nothing would make her forgo that moment.

Vaguely she became aware of Ella's enquiring gaze. What had she been saying? Something about dinner. The very thought of food sickened her, but she forced herself to concentrate. 'How about steak and onions? Oh, definitely!' she said brightly.

Ella was regarding her oddly and she wondered if she had overdone her enthusiasm in the matter of suggestions. 'But you said lamb chops just a moment ago. What *is* the matter with you, Christine?' Ella shot her what Christine privately termed one of her sickeningly sentimental glances. 'I know—you're in love! You must be. And I don't know that I can blame you. Myself, I never had much time for men with beards, but he's a nice lad all the same.'

Gavin! She was speaking about Gavin! Thank heaven the sharp eyes hadn't ferreted out the truth.

'Not like Kevin, of course,' came the quick tones, 'but of course you wouldn't have a chance there, not when he's already bespoken—or so they say.'

Christine had an impulse towards hysteria. Bespoken!— what a funny old-fashioned word. The next moment the laughter turned to heartache, a dull ache there was no assuaging. No, she hadn't a chance there, never, never, never! Abruptly she got up and fled the room before the tears came.

CHAPTER SEVEN

LYING sleepless in bed that night, Christine tried in vain to keep her thoughts from straying endlessly back to Kevin. It was no use; the dark intelligent face rose before her mental vision, eyes cool and alert—and definitely accusing. How could she have fallen in love, blindly, hopelessly, with a man who regarded her as a usurper, and as if that weren't enough, a man who was to marry someone else! Forget him, put him out of your mind, she told herself, keep busy.

Busy doing what? Ella, although inclined to be friendly towards her, didn't welcome help in her kitchen, except of course when there was a special load of work to be got through, such as on the day of the Hunt breakfast. How about outside tasks, then? There must be something she could do, like checking the boundaries looking for a break in the long line of eight-barred sheep fences. Perhaps Laurie might even agree to letting her help to draft the cattle. She liked riding Brownie, well as much as one could enjoy riding such a phlegmatic mount. Not to be compared with her earlier horse-riding activities, of course, but it was something to do. Maybe it wouldn't be long before she got her nerve back to ride a mount like Trooper, to take the high jumps once again with the old careless exhilaration.

Once again Kevin's mocking face flashed across the screen of her mind. She could almost hear the quiet sardonic tones, 'But you don't ride!' One day she would prove him wrong, one day. Dreams ... for deep down she knew there was still the grey area, the mental block in her mind which she couldn't seem to conquer. But I'm making progress with the people here, she comforted herself. Fred has been good to me from the start and Ella is coming around slowly, but I'll make her like me yet. She's rather nice once you get past her off-putting manner. Then there's Jan.

Unconsciously she sighed. Jan and Kevin, she thought bitterly, should get together. They both have the mistaken notion that merely because I happen to have been born not bad-looking I inveigled Laurie into staying on to work for me at Glendene. Jan tries not to let me see she's wildly jealous, but she gives herself away every time, insisting on following us everywhere we go even if Laurie is only showing me a fleece in the woolshed or telling me where to put the bridle away in the stables. If only Jan knew how wrong she is in her suspicions! I'm sure she never used to come over here so often before I came here. Luckily Laurie doesn't seem to realise how she feels about me.

The next day she put a suggestion of riding around the boundary fences to Laurie, and to her surprise he seemed grateful for the offer.

'I would enjoy the ride,' she told him, but deep down she knew that today she would grasp at any opportunity that would take her away from the house when Kevin came to collect Trooper and take him to Mata-Rangi.

'That's great,' Laurie told her. 'I'm having trouble with the pump down in the gully, so I'll leave you to it.' He grinned. 'Sure you can open and close the gates on horseback?'

'I'll manage. I'm a farm girl now, remember?'

'Right. Just keep your eyes peeled for any stragglers, steers or sheep that look as though they've strayed away from the main bunch.'

She raised her hand in a mock salute. 'Just as you say, Boss!'

A little later she caught Brownie, flung the sheepskin on his broad back, then put on the saddle and adjusted the girth. Presently she was following a track leading towards the hill paddocks above, carefully pulling the wire loop over each gate when she had passed through the opening.

At last she reached a vast paddock with its grazing steers and she cantered on. Out here in the immensity of green where the wind blew fresh and free and the only sound was the chiming notes of a tui somewhere in the bush-filled gully below, a little of the anxieties and frustrations that bedevilled her fell away. Some lines from verses written by the New Zealand poet James K. Baxter she had been reading a few days previously drifted through her mind.

> 'Upon the upland road
> Ride easy, stranger,
> Surrender to the sky
> Your heart of anger.'

Remembering the purpose of her ride, she pulled Brownie to a slower gait as she followed the fenceline. As she patrolled another hill paddock and another it seemed to her that each was more steep than the last. Uncle Ben must have kept his fences in first-class order, she reflected, for she could see nothing untoward, only the sheep dotted as closely as daisies, nibbling the short grass. Soon, however, she found she was mistaken, for a small group of woolly sheep were clearly on the wrong side of the boundary fence. It took her some time to guide the stragglers back through the gap. Now the problem was how to prevent them escaping once again. Looking around, she could see only a few low bushes, but it was something. She broke off some branches of tea-tree and wedged them in the gap as a temporary measure.

Engrossed in her task, it was not until she climbed back into the saddle that she caught sight of the rider below. Laurie probably, she thought, coming to join her. Laurie riding Trooper? That was odd, as hadn't he told her that the hunter was never used for farm work? *But he was no longer her uncle's horse.*

Her heart seemed to jump into her mouth. It was Trooper's new owner who was riding the hunter. Kevin sat his mount as though horse and rider were one. Even as she watched, the big grey, disdaining the gate, sailed through the air to land on the other side of a barbed fence. Then Trooper was moving at a gallop, clearing yet another fence, dropping pace to climb a steep slope, taking a worn sheep-track winding up the hill that she herself had travelled a short while since. *He was coming to find her.* What else?

Immediately she panicked. It was possible that he might not yet have sighted her and if she dropped down on the other side of the hill ... She dug her heels into Brownie and they moved down the steep slope into the filtered light of native trees and the lacy umbrella-like fronds of tall pungas. Now she was out of his view and safe, or so she hoped. Nevertheless she continued to urge Brownie on down the winding bush track, not daring to glance back for fear of seeing Kevin in swift pursuit. She couldn't have told why she was fleeing from him, she only knew she must escape him, and if she were lucky——

She wasn't! His cry of 'Christine!' was borne towards her on the wind. A quick glance over her shoulder revealed horse and rider coming over the crest of the hill. He must have seen her after all. Still under that wild compulsion to evade him at all costs, she urged Brownie on with a sharp kick. Taken by surprise, the mount leaped forward, to stumble over a concealed tree root in the damp leafmould underfoot, and Christine went flying through the air to land on her head and roll ignominiously down the slope for a few feet. A fallen tree blocked the way and she lay still for a moment, gasping for breath and fighting the black miasma of terror that enveloped her senses. She was back, back on another hilly slope—or was she? Realisation came slowly back. Where was she? Dazed and trembling, she realised that she was being held by someone, her head cradled in strong arms. A man was kneeling at her side and vaguely she was aware of two horses grazing nearby.

She made an effort to rise, but a voice said, 'Take it easy. Wait a minute.' Realisation came back with a rush. Kevin! In the dreamy state of bliss in which she found herself she would have been content to wait for ever. She closed her eyes and tried to spin out the magic moment, but the ordinary everyday part of her mind refused to co-operate. Instead it reminded her that all of this wasn't *real*, not the way she wanted it to be, that was, that he was merely acting in the way any man would in similar circum-stances. He didn't even like her particularly—on the con-trary—and she had no right, no right at all, to be feeling so ecstatically happy in his arms. She opened her eyes to catch the very real anxiety in the blue eyes of the man regarding her.

'Christine!' The note of concern in his usual offhand tones was almost too good to believe. 'I thought you were never coming out of it. You took a tumble down the hill, must have flaked out for a while.'

Christine promptly closed her eyes again. If she didn't let on ... but it was no use. He would find out in a minute or so that she hadn't been concussed at all, merely badly shaken, that she was only pretending and, God help her, enjoying the experience more than she had enjoyed anything in all her life. Christine, who up till now had always scorned feminine affectations, heard herself saying faintly the time-honoured phrase, 'Where am I?'

He bent over her, so close she could feel his breath on her face as he wiped her forehead. A surreptitious glance showed her the white handkerchief was blood-stained, probably from scratches she had sustained in her fall. 'You're not too far away from the house, don't worry about it.'

The look of solicitude on his lean bronzed face was worth the tumble down the hill, definitely. Aloud she murmured, 'Of all the stupid accidents!' Once again she made an effort to get up and was immediately held closer. 'Now don't hurry it, take your time.'

Had he known, she had already done that! Honesty prevailed and she smiled shakily up at him. 'I'm all right, just winded for a minute.'

'You're sure?' Reluctantly he released her and with the utmost tenderness helped her to her feet. Who would have believed that Kevin King—sorry, my mistake, Hawke— could treat her with such concern? He was still regarding her solicitously. 'No headache, no broken bones?'

At this she laughed aloud. Suddenly it was easy to laugh on this champagne day with Kevin's sympathetic voice in her ears. 'Can you imagine anyone really getting hurt on Brownie?'

The concern lingered in his expression. 'It's happened before. Sometimes the stupidest accidents come along out of the blue. It's not always the high jump that causes the trouble!'

'Don't I know it?' At his startled glance she hastily recovered herself. What was she saying? 'Accidents, I mean, not just riding ones. Poor old Brownie, she must have wondered what had happened when I baled out. I think she stumbled.'

'Not like Brownie to do a thing like that. She knows these sheep trails every foot of the way and she's as sure-footed as they come.'

Christine didn't answer. There was no doubt he was a difficult man to put anything over. She might have known he wouldn't believe her. 'I——' The scene swayed mistily around her and this time she knew it was for real. Kevin's voice seemed to be coming from a distance. 'No use telling me you're okay when you look as white as that all of a sudden. Better give it a few minutes before we take off again.'

The moment of dizziness passed, leaving her feeling oddly weak.

'Maybe you're right.' They dropped down on a grassy patch in the filtered sunshine while their mounts grazed quietly nearby. Overhead in a leafy tree, the tui burst forth in a cascade of bell-like notes.

Christine pushed the hair back from her forehead. The scratches seemed to have stopped bleeding, so they could not have been very deep. 'I'm okay now, honestly.'

'Good!' Kevin was resting on an elbow, turning on her the full impact of those alert eyes. 'Why were you running away from me?'

She tried for lightness. 'Running away? I don't know what you mean.'

'Don't you?' He was dangerously close to her, judging by the way in which her pulses were racing. He said softly, 'We got away to a bad start, you and I. We could begin all over again——'

'The way you think about me taking over from Laurie?' The words were out before she could stop them. 'Getting him to stay on with me. You were wrong about that, you know.' Her tone was low, almost incoherent. 'What you're thinking, I mean.'

He was regarding her narrowly. 'Really? Tell me then,

just how did you get around him to change his mind so quickly, other than the usual way, I mean?'

Her face flamed. 'You still think that about me? Well, you're wrong! You always have been! Would you believe me if I told you——'

His gaze took in the tumbled fair hair, the pale face and shadowed eyes. 'Looking as you do, even today, bloodstains and all,' he sent her an unreadable glance, 'you'll have to work hard to convince me——'

'Don't trouble yourself!' she cried angrily, and leaped to her feet. Oh, he was hateful, hateful! To think that she had been tempted to confide in him, to take a chance that in this new mood of concern for her he would believe her. How glad she was that she hadn't yielded to the insidious spell of bush and silence and being alone with him. 'You can think what you like!' She moved towards the grazing horses. 'Come on, Brownie, on your toes, it's time to get moving.'

Lazily Kevin rose to his full height. 'Just what I was about to suggest myself—want me to give you a leg up?'

'Please.' Her voice was tight with suppressed anger, but she placed a foot on his outstretched hand and jumped lightly up on to the saddle.

She pulled on a rein and as Brownie plodded up the narrow winding sheep track she found herself thinking longingly of her white show-jumper back home in England. Had she been riding Misty she would have been up and over the rise, heading down the steep inclines, way ahead of Kevin on his big grey. The next moment she reminded herself that all that was in the past; today she must content herself with Brownie's pedestrian pace while Kevin, close behind, attempted to slow Trooper's prancing steps to the farm hack's ambling gait.

When they were over the rise the mounts took the descent over the hill, Brownie leading the way. Then at last they were on smoother ground and Kevin was opening farm gates, waiting while she rode through. As they went on in angry silence Christine told herself that the only bright spot in this disastrous day was that Kevin believed her to be a learner rider, and wondered why his opinion should matter so much.

As to what she thought of him ... She caught her lip in her teeth. Oh, he was willing to start again, he had said, which meant he would overlook her supposed short-comings, forgive her. He actually seemed to think that his offer would make up for everything, including his complete lack of trust in her. How could he? For no reason that she could think of tears pricked her eyelids.

They were approaching the homestead when she said belatedly, 'Did you want to see me about something today? Or were you just trying out Trooper at a full gallop?'

'Both, actually. Know something? That's not a bad restaurant in town, the one by the traffic lights in the main street. Might even put on a floor show tonight if we're lucky.'

A curious thrill shot through her. Was this an invitation? She could scarcely believe it. She said carefully, 'Are you saying you want me to go out with you for a meal?'

'You could put it that way.' His smile was doing things to her resolutions, but she mustn't let him affect her like this. All she had to do was to steel herself to indignant recollection of his *real* feelings towards her, think hard about Wendy and her approaching birthday celebration and, most important of all, wrench her gaze aside.

'Sorry, but I've got a date tonight,' Refusing his invitation was harder to do than she would have imagined. Already regrets were fast crowding in on her.

'Is that right?' His unreadable glance puzzled her. 'Oh well,' he drawled carelessly, 'it's up to you.'

The dull heavy feeling inside her was still there, but she made her voice casual. 'Gavin said it was a good place to go for a meal.'

'It's also,' he observed dryly, 'the only restaurant in town.' The blue eyes were alive with a wicked gleam that made her wonder a little, but he made no suggestion for another date. The truth was he seemed not to care one way or the other. Not like herself, with this overwhelming sense of regret.

The feeling stayed with her as later in the day she got ready for the outing, slipping over her head the creamy Indian muslin blouse with its low scooped neckline that set off to advantage the lightly-tanned throat, fastening the gay cotton skirt that swirled around her ankles, tying the cords of her light-coloured sandals. Afterwards she went through the motions of applying make-up to her face, then stared into the mirror without really seeing her reflection. If only ... somehow the fleeting satisfaction of paying Kevin back in his own coil for his high-handed treatment of her ever since the day of her arrival here, was a hollow triumph. The betraying thought crowded everything else from her mind. If only she could have accepted his invitation today, how differently she would be feeling at this moment!

The double note of door chimes shattered her musing and snatching up her small gold evening bag she made her way to the lounge room. She smiled a welcome to Gavin and his face lighted up. 'Wow-ee!' he said on a long breath. There was no doubting his genuine appreciation of her appearance. It was plain to read in the twinkling eyes.

The next moment she became aware that Fred, who had been sunk in his favourite armchair as he watched television, had turned and was gazing towards her, his lined face wearing an expression of warm admiration. Christine, however, was accustomed to such masculine homage and took little notice. 'Come to that,' she said laughingly to Gavin, 'you look a little different tonight yourself.' Indeed, with his unruly dark hair slicked down into smooth waves, beard trimmed, and wearing a crimson velveteen jacket and matching floral shirt and well-pressed slacks, she scarcely recognised the rather nondescript-looking young man whom she was accustomed to seeing in working clothes and dust-smeared white coat.

Fred sent the younger man a friendly wink. 'Now see you take good care of her, young man.'

'You do look nice tonight, Christine,' Ella had come into the room. 'What I'd give to be your age with all your advantages and looking the way you do!'

If she only knew! Christine wrenched her mind back to Fred's smiling tones. 'And see you bring her home at a reasonable hour,' he called to Gavin with mock severity.

'That's up to her.' Gavin took her arm and they stepped out into the still warm darkness.

As he opened the passenger door of the light van Christine paused, looking around her. 'They're incredibly black, the nights here. I've never been in darkness like this, but then I guess I've never been far away from city lights before.'

'It's got its advantages.' He threw an arm around her waist, but moved by an impulse she couldn't define she slipped from his grasp and got into the van.

Soon they were out on the road and moving towards the blurred outlines of the hills ahead. 'How long have you been at Glendene?' he enquired.

'Only a few weeks.'

'Pretty good going.' He threw her a sideways grin.

She turned towards him, her voice puzzled. 'What do you mean?'

'Only that I've been hearing things about you and the reason you came out here all the way from London. I got the idea at first that you were out here for a holiday. You know? The usual story, working girl takes off for the other side of the world to take a look around while she has a working holiday, then I got the real story.' He threw her a laughing glance. 'Congratulations! I gather you got off here to a bad start, but in no time at all you had them all eating out of your hand. It sure didn't take you long for you to get them all on your side—me too!'

Bless you, Gavin! she thought. Here at last was someone who was unprejudiced towards her, a newcomer to the district like herself, someone to whom the local gossip meant nothing. To Gavin the passing of a property to her meant little. He was interested in her as a person, not merely as an object of speculation and suspicion. In this closely knit community she still felt she was regarded as a scheming, self-seeking blonde who was only too anxious to hold on to the inheritance fate had tossed her way. Oh, she might have endeared herself to Ella and Fred, but Kevin's opinion of her remained unchanged, nothing could alter that and, no use in denying it to herself any longer, he was the only one who mattered.

Gavin's gay tones broke in on her musing. 'Tell me, what was your secret?'

'Aha,' she murmured mysteriously.

'Never mind, I can answer that one! Whatever happened beforehand, once folks got to know you they couldn't help falling for you.'

'Flattery,' she said wryly, 'will get you nowhere. Anyway,' she went on as Kevin's strong features rose before her mental vision, 'it wasn't quite as simple as that.'

'It seemed to be as far as Laurie was concerned,' the light teasing tones protested, 'and you can't get away from it, from what I could make out he was the one most concerned.'

'Oh, Laurie . . .' To change the subject she said quickly, 'Tell me about yourself. You haven't been here long either?'

'That's right.' His arm still rested around her shoulders, his gaze was on the fragment of road ahead illuminated in the beam of the headlights. 'I'd got through my finals at last and was looking around for a place when a vacancy for a vet turned up down here. I come from the North and it's quite a change for me, real horse country. Down this way hunting and polo are a way of life and the old sheep stations dotted around the hills are quite something. Some of them have been worked by three generations of the same family. Riding happens to be a hobby of mine and the horses here are tough, bred and trained on rugged hills— they could take on just about anything, I reckon. The same goes for the riders. It takes a fairly proficient rider to clear the high barbed fences on the Gisborne hills. Taken all round I guess that this place has got it all, my sort of country,' his arm tightened around her, 'my sort of girl.'

Because mention of the Hunt brought back thoughts of Kevin she said quickly, 'You really like living here, then?'

His swift sideways glance took in the profile of the girl at his side, the small nose and softly-curving lips, strands of pale blonde hair moving on her forehead in the night breeze. 'Now I do!'

She laughed and he went on to recount amusing anecdotes concerning his daily work and the variety of animals he was called upon to treat. For Christine time went by swiftly and soon the lights of an isolated farmhouse on high slopes gave way to long avenues of suburban homes. Presently they were turning into the city's main street and half way down the lighted area Gavin drew in to a parking lot. As she stood on the pavement waiting as he locked the van, Christine's gaze went high above the street where a small model of a sailing ship was outlined against a dark sky.

Gavin had come to stand at her side. 'A model of Captain Cook's ship the *Endeavour*, just for your information,' he told her.

'I know.' She had no desire to hear about the sailing vessel that had landed on alien shores over a century ago. It reminded her too forcibly of a man she was determined to put out of her mind.

They strolled through a tastefully-decorated craft shop, took a flight of carpeted stairs, then Gavin led her into a dimly lighted restaurant. As a waiter guided them towards a corner table a lean masculine figure rose lazily at their approach and even in the dim blue lights gleaming from pottery lanterns Christine could glimpse the satirical amusement in Kevin's eyes. Taken aback, she flung a startled glance over her shoulder towards her escort. 'You didn't tell me it was to be a party for dinner tonight!'

'Didn't I?' The expression of adoring indulgence on his pleasant young face was all at once vaguely irritating. 'What difference does it make? Anyway, it's not a party, just Andrea and Kevin.'

Kevin! What was Gavin saying? 'I happened to run into him in town today and we decided to join forces for a night out.'

She felt hot with humiliation and her thoughts milled in confusion. To think that she had actually imagined he was inviting her out to a dinner date alone with him! Had congratulated herself on having scored a victory over him when all the time ... Now she knew the reason for the mocking light in his eyes earlier in the day. Worst of all, he would know only too well what she was thinking. Somehow she had to conceal her surprise at seeing him here, him and Andrea. She *couldn't* love him, a man like that, but deep down she knew that in spite of everything, she did, fool that she was.

'Hi, you two,' Kevin was saying easily. 'Andrea, you know Christine, don't you?'

Christine nodded. She had a swift impression of a wide smiling mouth, flashing dark eyes, an air of animation. 'We got acquainted the day of the Hunt breakfast at——' She broke off in some confusion. Why must she stumble? She could have handled this conversation so much more easily had she been prepared beforehand. Nevertheless, the words had to be said, even under Kevin's watchful glance, 'At my place.'

'Is that where it was?' Andrea appeared to have already lost interest in her. 'I'd forgotten, there was such a crowd there that day.'

'Evening, Christine.' Kevin flashed his devastating smile, his strong teeth very white against the tan. 'Feeling better now?'

'All the time.' As she seated herself at the small table Andrea leaned forward. 'I've heard about you, of course.' She beamed a wide smile towards Christine, a smile which somehow lost itself in Kevin's direction. 'Everyone for miles around the place has been talking about you arriving from England.'

Was this a deliberately cruel thrust aimed at her? Christine wondered. She raised her clear gaze to Andrea's dark eyes. 'Why?'

'Why not?' Gavin appeared to see nothing significant in the conversation. 'It isn't every day of the week a lovely girl like Christine comes twelve hundred miles all by herself to take up residence on the other side of the world! Right, Kevin?' he eyed the other man cheerfully.

Christine's glance went to the man seated opposite her at the table and in that instant she was aware of something, a life-force, powerful, beyond her control, that flashed between them. With an effort of will she wrenched her gaze aside. Her emotions in a tumult, she forced herself to listen for his response. No doubt, she told herself, he wouldn't miss such an opportunity of demonstrating his own lack of enthusiasm in regard to the girl from England.

The next moment she found she was mistaken. He merely inclined his dark head and applied himself to the menu the waiter had handed to him. Christine did her best to ignore him, she really did, but all the time her gaze was running down the items on the printed sheet she was disconcertingly aware of him.

The meal was delicious, the food tasteful and attractively served and the local wine light and enjoyable. Somehow, however, although outwardly calm as she chatted and smiled, Christine was scarcely conscious of the food she was eating. Almost she was grateful to the dark girl seated at her side as Andrea kept up her lively stream of chatter. What matter that the talk was confined to sporting events, friends and acquaintances known only to her and Kevin? At least Andrea's easy flow, punctuated with loud bursts of laughter, made up for her own lack of conversation. Not that she was as a rule lacking in light talk, but there was something about Kevin's presence that threw her into a state of confusion—and that when he had scarcely addressed two words to her! The man seemed to have that effect on her. Could it be something to do with the half-mocking smile that touched his lips whenever their glances chanced to meet? She would have to do something about

the influence he seemed to have on her emotions and get
the better of it—if she could!

As a group of three young guitarists on a small stage
broke into a foot-tapping rhythm, she was aware of Gavin
at her side, his bearded young face close to her own. 'Shall
we dance?'

'If you like.' Soon they were moving to the tempo of the
latest hit tune and presently other couples joined them on
the small cleared area of the room. Later when they made
their way back to their table they found Andrea and Kevin
apparently deeply absorbed in some topic of their own. It
was always the same when those two were together, Christine thought crossly. Kevin's dark head was inclined attentively towards Andrea as he listened in apparent interest to
something she was saying in a low tone.

Andrea glanced up as Christine seated herself once more
at the table. 'I suppose you danced to that tune ages ago in
London?'

'No, it only came out a few weeks ago. It topped the hit
parades all over the country and I heard it on the radio, but
I've never danced to it until tonight.'

No need to explain that she had first heard the lilting
notes from her little transistor on a table by her bedside as
she lay helpless in a hospital bed recovering from injuries
she had sustained in a riding accident. She brought her
mind back to Andrea's penetrating tones.

'I don't suppose you'll be staying long anyway?' There
was something in the intent glance that lent significance to
the casual words. 'I mean, there's nothing here for you, not
really, not after living in a city like London?'

Careful, Christine, that's a loaded question. Why did
Andrea care so much about her movements? 'I haven't
decided yet how long I'll be here.' A safe answer that gave
nothing away.

'But you can't really be enjoying it,' Andrea persisted.
'There's nothing for you to do, is there?'

'She doesn't need to do anything.' Once again Gavin
came to her rescue. He grinned engagingly. 'It's enough to

have her around, you know? To look at!'

To her relief Andrea abandoned the subject of herself. It was funny how the older girl somehow contrived to make Christine feel useless, inept. Funny and somehow dispiriting. If it wasn't for being determined to stay here until she had proved to Kevin how mistaken he had been in his snap judgment of her, she would leave immediately and return to London. Was that what Andrea wanted? But why? It was all very puzzling. If Andrea imagined that Kevin had any particular interest in the girl from England, she mused bleakly, she couldn't be more mistaken.

After a short interval she danced once again with Gavin and as they returned to the table she made a pretence of chatting gaily, but she was only half aware of what she was saying. She couldn't seem to wrench her attention from the two people seated at the table. Andrea's intimate glance was raised to Kevin's smiling face. He could smile for Andrea, she thought crossly, a real smile, warm, friendly, companionable, not the twisted grin he seemed to keep just for her.

Close on the thought came another. Kevin would feel duty bound to ask her to dance, just as she would be duty bound to accept. So why feel this wild excitement merely because he had risen to his feet and was moving in her direction. 'Shall we?'

A little later they were moving to the infectious rhythm. Then the melody changed to a slower tempo and soft Maori voices rose in the cadence of a haunting love-song, an age-old native chant new to Christine. It was then that Kevin caught her close and they moved together in slow conventional dance steps. Christine, in a state of bemusement, was scarcely aware that other couples had left the floor and there was only Kevin and herself moving together in a languorous unfamiliar world of dim lights and beguiling melody. She could have danced on for ever, close in his arms. Then all at once the plaintive Maori voices died away, the beat changed back to modern tempo and for Christine, once again the excitement took over. Her eyes were shining and strands of blonde hair were flying back from her flushed face. Could it be that dancing with an antagonist, someone you hated—well, *had* hated—could spark this exhilarating rapture that was like being in love? Love ... But you are in love with him. Who are you trying to fool?

At last the music crashed to a close and the spell was broken. Breathless she stood motionless, aware of Kevin's face lighted with some inner excitement, caught his low exultant laugh. The next moment he had taken her hand in his warm strong clasp and he was leading her back towards their table.

Andrea took in Christine's flushed and smiling face. 'Quite an exhibition!' The other girl's flashing smile held a hint of malice.

Gavin's glance went from one girl to the other. 'What do you think of Maori guitar music anyway, Christine?'

She was still in a state of bemusement. 'Love it!'

'That's good,' he grinned, 'because they're tuning up again. Shall we give everyone a lead?'

'If you like.' She pushed the hair back from her hot face and went with him. As they strolled on to the dance floor and began moving to the insistent beat she thought: He's nice. I feel happy and at ease with Gavin, not like that—that disturbing, devastatingly attractive Kevin Hawke! She matched her steps to Gavin's swaying movements. I must have been crazy to let Kevin affect me that way, she thought. Blame the Maori music!

CHAPTER EIGHT

As the weeks slipped by Christine endeavoured to put from her mind all thoughts of the party to be given by Kevin's parents for Wendy's coming of age. 'Coming of age', she told herself, was the operative phrase. To dwell on the announcement to be made on that evening was only to invite heartache, for there was no denying any longer that she loved Kevin and she always would. Pain swift and unexpected caught at her heart. She had thought she hated him and all the time ... she pressed her lips together to stop the trembling.

When had it changed, the feeling she had had for him? Or had it been that way from the beginning only she hadn't recognised it, hadn't known that a violent antagonism could be the start of love? Her mind went back to his punishing kiss in the shadows of the old Maori meeting house, the moment out in the far hills when she had lain in his arms, the night in the restaurant. How could you love a man who despised you? she wondered drearily. The answer came unbidden: How could you help it? The one comfort she could hug to herself was that he would never know, that at least she could salvage from the hopeless position into which she had got herself.

Perhaps the reason she spent so much time with Gavin, she reflected, was because his friendly uncomplicated companionship was a balm to the heartache she tried so hard to conceal. During the past weeks his white-coated figure had become a familiar sight at Glendene and Christine was aware that Ella's sharp eyes, ever on the scent of a romance, had not missed the frequency of his visits. Then all at once there was no evading the date on the calendar.

She knew that on this night of all nights she must play her part were she to keep her secret. Appearances would help, of course, and she would have need of all the confidence she could muster. She washed her hair, setting it in big rollers, and when it was dry brushed out the fine strands.

When at last she could no longer delay the matter of getting ready for the evening ahead she went to her room and took from the wardrobe a deceptively simple black dress. It had been thrown into her travel bag at the last moment, as she hadn't really expected an opportunity would arise deep in the New Zealand countryside to wear the dress, but now ... Black, she thought on a sigh, sort of symbolic, but what matter the colour when the dress did something for her—a lot really, even though her complexion was no longer London-pale. A touch of lip gloss, a smear of turquoise on her eyelids and a quick upward flick of the mascara brush on her lashes was all the make-up she needed.

Despite the shadows around her eyes she knew that tonight she looked her best. The translucent golden-tan acquired in the long hours spent out of doors during the past weeks suited her. Not that *he* would notice, she mused bleakly, for clearly he had schooled himself from the beginning against any appeal her beauty might have for him. Out of the past a conversation between them flashed back to mind. It had been one of the many occasions when his attitude of mocking contempt had stung her into defiant retaliation.

'Don't you like girls?' she had challenged him teasingly. There had been no answering smile in his level-eyed stare. 'Oh yes, I like girls.'

Some devil inside her had prompted her to go on, 'But not blondes?'

'Sure,' his voice was disinterested, 'I like blondes.'

Unexpectedly a shaft of hurt stabbed her. '*But not me?*'
'I didn't say that.'

'You didn't need to, did you?' and before he could answer she had flung away. To think that before she came to Gisborne she had believed that everyone in the district had a reputation for friendliness, that they would go out of their way to help you. Not so. One thing, at last she had succeeded in getting through to Kevin but somehow there was no joy in the thought. What had she expected from him anyway? Compliments on her beauty? She must have been crazy!

Dispiritedly she turned aside. There she went again, losing herself in thoughts of him. It did no good at all but merely spoiled the pleasures of the moment. With a sigh she bent to pick up from the bureau an attractively wrap-

ped gift she had selected for Wendy's birthday, a beautifully printed art book featuring the life and works of the
artist Renoir. Absently she leafed through the pages.
Would Wendy be able to keep up her interest in art and
handcrafts once she found herself mistress of the old
homestead with its staff of outdoor workers and endless
calls upon her time? Close on the thought came another. If
it were me I wouldn't ever want anything else but to be his
wife and bear his children, be with him every day and—she
caught her breath—every night. The anguish of longing
was almost more than she could bear and desperately she
tried to force her thoughts aside. Think of Gavin. She could
hear his van coming up the slope outside the window. It's
only for an evening, she consoled herself; surely one could
endure anything for a few hours.

She was waiting in the lounge when Jan and Laurie came
into the room. Almost immediately Gavin arrived to join
them.

'You look fantastic in that dress, Christine!' For the first
time the other girl's gaze was free of the jealous glint
Christine had come to expect. 'Doesn't she, Gavin?'

'Sure does.' For once he appeared at a loss for words,
but his deep warm look was a tribute to her loveliness.

One thing, Christine told herself wryly, she had to be
thankful for and that was Jan's change of attitude towards
her. Jan could be agreeable when she wished, and one had
no need of a crystal ball to see that Christine as Gavin's
special girl-friend was far more acceptable to Jan than the
stranger from England whom Laurie treated with an affec-
tionate regard sufficient to make any girl-friend crazy with
jealousy—any girl who wasn't aware of her true position
here, that was. It was a relief not to be written off by the
other girl as a man-chaser as well as a property-grabber.

'You look rather special yourself,' she tossed the com-
pliment back. Indeed tonight Jan appeared to have an inner
glow. Maybe it was something to do with the gold and
bronze tonings of her cool caftan falling softly around her
slim figure, but more likely, Christine mused wistfully, the

reason was Laurie's arm thrown around Jan's shoulders, his blond head bent close to her dark hair. No, Jan had no need to worry over where Laurie's affections lay. Lucky Jan, to be so sure of her man!

Later they moved out to the verandah, chatting idly and watching a feathery mass of pink in the western sky slowly deepen to a blaze of crimson. Laurie was handing around drinks, beer for the men, sherry for the girls, and Christine, sipping her wine, reflected that tonight could have been a fun evening had things been different.

A haze of evening had fallen over the hills when at length Laurie laid down the guitar he had been strumming. 'Time to go, everyone!'

'Right!' Laughingly Gavin pulled Christine to her feet and they moved with the others out into the yard where Fred and Ella were getting into their own car.

Because she was dreading the function ahead the journey through the growing dusk seemed all too short. To Christine it seemed no time at all until they were turning the last bend in the road, and ahead the homestead was a blaze of lights against its dark shelterbelt of trees. They took the winding drive up to pull up at the woolshed and Gavin guided his van to a space among the cluster of trucks, station waggons, cars and Land Rovers parked haphazardly on the grass.

Soon they were making their way through groups of guests, climbing the high step and moving inside the great shed. Christine was aware of banks of punga ferns and greenery arranged in corners of the room and of garish overhead bulbs sheathed in pink paper. Hay bales were scattered around the walls and at the end of the room a man was seated at the piano while three youths took up guitars.

Gavin guided her through the throng and presently they were being greeted by Kevin's mother and father. As usual Marie Hawke was beautifully groomed. She wore a sequined dress and smiled a welcome to Christine, then Gavin. Kevin's father, looking incredibly changed in his evening suit, took Christine's hand in a strong grasp. Feeling the roughness of his work-weathered hand, she reflected that maybe he wasn't so changed after all.

'Kevin's somewhere around,' he was saying, and Christine felt herself relax. Only for a moment, however, then she was peering through the milling crowd in search of a lean masculine figure.

'Christine!' Guiltily she wondered how she could have overlooked Wendy who, she now realised, was regarding her with bright over-excited eyes. The flounces of the pink dress that trailed around her ankles concealed her disability and she appeared to be rapturously happy. Christine's voice said brightly, 'Happy birthday!' Her mind said, No wonder she's looking radiant tonight. Wouldn't you?

Vaguely she became aware of Mrs Hawke's friendly tones. 'Such a job we had getting the piano over from the house.' Then came Wendy's warm excited voice: 'So glad you could come tonight, Christine!' The next moment Gavin was piloting her among the chattering groups, two strangers among the crowd of guests who had known one another for many years. Presently the group on the makeshift stage began to pluck their throbbing guitars, the pianist's hands went to the keys and soon the cleared space in the centre of the shed was filled with a moving pattern of whirling couples. Christine moved automatically to the beat, but all the time her eyes searched the dancers. At last through a gap in the crowd she caught a glimpse of Kevin, and then wished she hadn't. Because of course he was with Andrea and as usual she was gazing up into his face, laughing and talking as if they were alone on the floor. Maybe to Andrea he *was* the only person in the big room who mattered. And that, she thought with bitter irony, makes three of us!

As the evening wore on Gavin made certain that he gave no other partner an opportunity to dance with her and Christine was content to leave it at that. If she couldn't be with Kevin what did it matter who she danced with?

She was standing beside Gavin between dances and the

band had just broken into a pop tune when out of a corner of her eye she was aware of Kevin striding purposefully through the crowd in her direction. All at once she panicked. 'Gavin——' She hoped he hadn't guessed the reason for the sudden peremptory note in her voice, but if so he gave no sign. He simply took her hand in his and hurried on to the floor.

Dance after dance . . . Christine's hair was loose around her face and her cheeks were flushed. Then it was supper time and long trestle tables were brought in. They were piled with cold meats, fish and savouries, and great wooden platters were filled with rice and green salads. Crystal bowls held fruit salad and on flat glass plates were piled fluffy pavlovas, white and crisp and decorated with whipped cream and slices of the silvery-green delicately flavoured kiwi-fruit. It was delicious food that Christine might have enjoyed at any other time. Now it was an effort for her to make a pretence of eating.

Supper was all but at an end when Kevin, seated at the head of the table with Wendy, rose to his feet and a hush fell over the chattering crowd. 'Folks, I'd like to propose a toast——' glasses were filled from decanters scattered along the tables, 'to Wendy on her coming of age!' He smiled towards the girl seated at his side. 'I guess you all know that that's what the show tonight is all about?'

As glasses were raised Wendy, her pale face glowing, smilingly acknowledged the toast. A thunderous clapping broke out, but Christine was scarcely aware of the calls of 'Happy birthday, Wendy!' that echoed around her. The thoughts chased one another through her distraught mind. It was like an unhappy dream, but it wasn't a dream and there was no escape. She was forced to sit here among the lighthearted crowd keeping the silly smile plastered on her face while all the while she must nerve herself for the blow that was about to fall—a blow that would put an end for ever to those foolish dreams of hers. She must have been crazy ever to have hoped that Kevin would one day come to love her as she loved him.

In a few minutes it would all be over and once the engagement was made public she would have to decide what to do. One part of her urged her to flight. She couldn't stay on here, playing a part, pretending she didn't care, that everything was just the same. Another impulse equally strong prompted her to stay. Just a few more weeks until the legal proceedings were completed and she had the bleak satisfaction of letting Kevin in on the truth. What she had let herself in for was heartbreak, no doubt of that, and she had done it with her eyes wide open. At least after he had gone out of her life, she thought forlornly, he would remember her as she really was and not as he imagined her to be at present, cold, grasping, insensitive. It wasn't much to look forward to, but it was *something*.

Lost in her thoughts all at once, she realised that Kevin's father had got to his feet. He was running a hand over bristly grey hair. 'Friends, I've got a surprise for you——'

Christine felt a stab of pain run through her and she braced herself for what was to come. 'As you all know, Wendy has no parents of her own and it's my pleasure to pass on the good news! The show tonight isn't just to mark her birthday. She wants me to be the one to let you know there's something else we're celebrating here tonight——'

To Christine the faces around her blurred out of focus and she felt sick in her stomach. Frantically she tried to pull herself together. What if anyone had noticed? Already she was aware of Andrea, seated beside her at the table and eyeing her closely. Quick, Christine, put the silly smile back on your face before you give yourself away altogether!

'It happens to be a farewell party too!' There was an attentive silence and the scene around her steadied. A farewell? Were Wendy and Kevin moving to another district to live, then?

A murmur of voices broke out and Mr Hawke held up a hand for silence. What was he saying now? The words were hazy as if coming from a distance. ' ... announce their engagement to be married quite soon.' Dimly she was aware of Andrea, who had turned her head and was watching *her* instead of the speaker. A black mist swirled around her and for a moment she slumped in her seat, but somehow she managed to struggle back to full awareness. She mustn't flake out now of all times.

When the thunder of applause had died away Mr Hawke went on, 'Wendy is going over to England to be married next month to a man she has known for a long time. Some of you may remember him—Bill Dailey? He worked at the Cook Hospital here for a while a couple of years ago. Now he's arranged for Wendy to go to England and they'll be married from his family place in Cornwall. I hear there's to be a honeymoon in Paris,' more wild applause, 'and—wait for it, folks—there's a good chance that before long Dr Dailey will be bringing Wendy back with him and taking up a practice right here on the east coast!' The last words were drowned in cheering and clapping and once again glasses were raised. Only Christine was silent, dazed and shaken. She was scarcely able to believe what she had just heard. All at once she realised that Andrea, her head sharply inclined towards her, was still regarding her curiously. 'Gave you a shock?' The red lips were curved in a smile, but the words were spiced with malice. 'Not quite what you were expecting to hear, was it? Nearly but not quite!'

The observation was so close to her own thoughts that she breathed an involuntary, 'No, not really,' then sat very still. So the other girl had noticed her distress and she, crazy idiot that she was, had betrayed herself.

'I thought you looked mighty relieved,' Andrea added.

Now Christine had got herself in hand, but it was too late. 'Relieved? What do you mean by that?'

'Oh, come on, you know what I mean. I'll give you three guesses! At one stage I thought you were going to pass out, you went as white as a sheet.' Suddenly Christine realised that Andrea had been drinking a lot during the evening. Her face was flushed and the words started to slur. 'Wouldn't have done you any good flaking out, because

Kevin wouldn't have been handy to carry you out in his arms. Poor Christine ... all wasted!'

She had a sick fear that the shrill tones might have carried above the clamour of voices around them. The next moment she wondered if Gavin, seated on the other side, had overheard the other girl's outburst, for he was leaning towards Andrea saying pleasantly, 'Hello, your glass is empty. Can't have that, you know, not tonight. I'll get you some champagne.'

The words had the effect of diverting Andrea's attention and she seemed to pull herself together, 'Oh, will you— thanks a lot, Gavin!'

Thank you, Gavin, echoed Christine, but she made the comment silently.

Throughout the remainder of time spent at the supper table the thought persisted. Andrea had noticed her distress, the undoubted pallor of her face. What if others had noticed too and drawn their own conclusions? A dismaying thought pierced her. Supposing that Andrea confided her own suspicions of Christine's feelings for Kevin to *him*? Surely she couldn't, she wouldn't ... but in her heart Christine was well aware that Andrea was perfectly capable of doing just that. She could imagine the jeering tones, 'Silly little thing, she's fallen for you in a big way!' She could almost hear their laughter. They seemed to her always to be laughing together, sharing some secret joke.

Presently everyone got up from the table to mill around Wendy, who tonight possessed a radiance that transformed the thin pale face.

'Isn't it all just wonderful!' she confided to Christine when at last she was able to push her way through the crowd gathered around the girl still seated at the head of the long table. 'I told you I had a secret! I was dying to tell you, but Kevin persuaded me to wait and make it a real surprise! This was the time to let everyone know, he said, and he was right, I guess.' She flashed a smile. 'He's usually right, don't you think?'

'Maybe.' Christine glanced across to Kevin. A glass held

in his hand, he was with a group of station owners. At that moment he caught her eye and his expression seemed to change and soften. Perhaps she hadn't imagined his look, because Wendy was saying, 'He likes you, you know.'

Likes! Once again pain stabbed her. Quickly she murmured, 'I'm so glad for you. A sort of fairy-tale romance with a happy ending!'

'Isn't it?' Fortunately Wendy hadn't caught the wistful note in her tone. 'Sometimes I can scarcely believe it myself!' The excitement in her voice died away. 'I've always loved Bill, I think I fell in love with him the moment I met him, but I didn't think he would ever feel that way about me. I didn't even think he cared enough to write me once he left here. He never *said* anything and I thought ... but he did write, the very day he arrived back in England. It was then that I started hoping, but I didn't breathe a word to anyone about how I felt about him. It was just as if I had something so precious, so kind of fragile, like when you hold a butterfly in your hand, that if I told anyone about it it wouldn't ever happen the way I wanted it to. Sounds silly, doesn't it?' Tears of happiness sparkled in her eyes. 'Do you know what I mean?'

Did she know? Aloud she murmured, 'I can imagine.' On an impulse she added, 'I'll come and see you in England after you're married.'

'After you're married,' Wendy echoed on a long sigh of content, 'doesn't it sound super!' The next moment her expression changed. 'But you'll be here!'

'No, I'll be back in England before too many months.' It was foolish to believe in miracles. Even if Kevin did at times have a tendresse for her, it would turn to amusement once he heard Andrea's version of her reaction to tonight's announcement.

'Oh! Somehow I never thought of you going back so soon.'

Her heart cried, I'd never never leave here if Kevin—— She sighed and pushed the thought away.

'I suppose, though,' Wendy was saying slowly, 'that London is your home.'

Home? An apartment in a crowded city? Home was here among the high hills with the man she loved.

She wrenched her mind back to the eager tones. 'You'll have to help me get ready for the trip, tell me what sort of clothes to take for an English summer. And Paris, can you imagine being in Paris with the man you love!'

Presently excited voices echoed around Wendy as other friends crowded near and Christine slipped away. The band had resumed the foot-tapping rhythm and couples were moving towards the dance floor. Once again as she moved with Gavin in time with the infectious beat, her eyes sought Kevin; she couldn't help it. No one could resist looking at him, she thought dreamily. He was so tall and erect with that air of distinction about him. He was with a group she recognised as members of the local Hunt Club, a man one couldn't help noticing—*couldn't help loving*, supplied her heart. A sudden hope rose within her. It could be that Andrea in her slightly befuddled state might already have forgotten Christine's moment of betrayal. Well, she *might*, and who knew, once the confirmation of the gift of Glendene came through, once he came to realise the sort of girl and really was . . . anyone could dream, couldn't they?

A scintillating swaying group obscured the masculine group for a moment and when she caught sight of Kevin once again her heart flipped. Andrea was weaving her way towards him, a champagne goblet in her hand, her high tones shriller than usual, piercing the murmur of voices and the lilting notes of the band. 'So there you are! I couldn't wait to tell you this bit of news . . . been looking for you all over. You'd never believe it!' She linked her arm in his and as they moved away together the remainder of the words were drowned in a sudden burst of music, but Christine had heard enough, more than enough. Against her volition her gaze was drawn back to Andrea and Kevin. They were standing together, and guess who was the subject of their evident amusement?

A sick feeling of dismay crowded in on her. What had she done? Right at this moment no doubt Andrea was making the most of Christine's involuntary confidence, telling him —her step faltered and swiftly she recovered herself—about stupid Christine who had had those ridiculous hopes of one day sharing his life. Had it been possible she would have fled the room right at this moment, gone somewhere, anywhere away from the amused gleam in Kevin's eyes. She had glimpsed it often enough in the past and this time he would have good reason for entertainment at her expense. She'd die, she would just die of mortification if she had to be alone with him ever again!

That evening she discovered she could play a part if she had to, and apart from that initial blunder she played it well. Apparently no one noticed anything untoward about her as she danced the hours away, sometimes with Gavin at other times with Laurie, but never, thank heaven, with Kevin. So far she had succeeded in avoiding him. On two occasions she had caught sight of his tall figure as he threaded his way through the crowd of guests in her direction, but swiftly she had got to her feet. A touch on Gavin's arm and they moved away together. A swift backward glance made her aware that Kevin had turned away and was retracing his steps. At least she wouldn't give him the satisfaction of quizzing her on that damning admission of hers. That much she could do, especially as Gavin clearly was only too anxious to be with her and no other partner for every moment of the time.

It was in the early hours of the morning when the band had paused for a break in the dancing that Mrs Hawke came hurrying over the floor to tap Gavin on the shoulder. 'Sorry to be the one to hand you the bad news, but Tim Armstrong has just rung through from the racing stud. Seems he wants you in a hurry. He said he wouldn't have troubled you at this time of the night, but his mare's in a bad way and needs you urgently.'

Gavin's face fell. 'Damn and blast!' he muttered. 'It would be tonight of all nights that his mare has chosen to foal. Trouble is Tim's pinning all of his hopes on that same foal and I can't let him down. Sorry, Christine,' his regretful glance lent meaning to the conventional words, 'I'll be back as soon as I can, but somehow,' he groaned, 'I can't see it being for an hour or two.'

'Don't worry,' she tried to hide the note of relief in her voice, 'it will all be breaking up before long.'

Still he lingered. 'You'll be all right?'

'Of course. Laurie and Jan will take me back with them.' As he turned reluctantly away she called, 'Ring me in the morning and let me know how you got on in the stables? If the foal is all right?'

'It had better be,' he flung over his shoulder, 'seeing I've got to tear off in the middle of things!' A twisted smile for Christine and he was striding away.

Above the babel of talk and laughter Christine realised that Mrs Hawke was saying something about the next number being the last dance of the evening, then the older woman left her.

Christine couldn't be more glad. Already the band had started up and she knew it wouldn't be long before she could make her escape. Then she saw Kevin once again moving towards her. Did the man never learn? Evidently he just couldn't wait to enjoy his victory over her. Something about his purposeful stride told her she must act quickly, and this time there was no Gavin to aid her escape. Swiftly she turned to a youth standing at her side. She had been half aware of his shy admiring glance throughout the evening and guessed he had lacked the courage to ask her to dance.

'Want to get up with me?' she smiled.

'Gee . . . did you mean it?'

Had it not been for her inner agitation she would have been amused by the expressions that chased one another across the boyish features—utter astonishment, disbelief, followed by an incredulous delight. When she next caught a glimpse of Kevin he was dancing with Andrea. Her own partner's face now wore an expression of intense concen-

tration, his youthful face red and perspiring. Nervousness?
Heat?

But she soon forgot him, her gaze drawn by a magnet to
Kevin and his partner. Even if Andrea hadn't informed him
of Christine's secret passion for him—she writhed in humiliation at the thought—even then he probably had only
approached her for a duty dance. Certainly at the moment
he appeared to be perfectly happy with Andrea.

At length the music crashed to a close and couples
turned and began moving in the direction of the open doorway. Christine pushed her way through the crowd and
made her farewells to Kevin's parents.

'Oh, Christine,' she was turning away when Mrs Hawke's
voice halted her, 'Kevin will see you home. He told me he
would.'

She stood frozen. 'There's no need, truly.' She felt as
though the smile she had worn all evening was becoming a
permanent fixture on her face. 'I'll be with Laurie and Jan.'

'That's all right, then. 'Night.'

A smiling group crowded around them and in the general
murmur of farewells and laughter Christine slipped away.
Stepping lightly down the high step, she hurried away from
the beam of light from above the woolshed door. The night
breeze tossed her hair back from her flushed face and
wrapped her dress around her as she went on, threading
her way between the vehicles clustered on dew-wet grass.

She reached the car at last and was about to open the
rear door when a dark shadow loomed up at her side and
an all-too-familiar voice said quietly, 'Wrong car, Christine.'

'Not for me it isn't!' Trapped, she swung around to face
him. Had he followed her from the woolshed or had he
been awaiting her arrival? Either way spelt disaster so far
as she was concerned.

She made a movement towards the door handle once
again and felt his hand, strong and purposeful, close over
hers. 'It is, you know. I'm taking you home.'

'That's news to me.' In the light of moving headlamps

she caught the quirk of his lips. 'I happen to be going with the others. There's no need for you to bother——'

'No bother. And as to Laurie and Jan...' He stood motionless, arms folded, looking down on her just as though he had all the time in the world. 'I had a word with them both a few minutes ago and I doubt if they'd appreciate your sacrifice——'

'*Sacrifice!* If you think——'

'Of course,' he tossed off carelessly, 'if you really want to wait around for them and play gooseberry——'

He had caught her neatly. To elect to go with the others at this stage would give a clear indication of the tension that existed between Kevin and herself, and that she couldn't risk. 'Oh, all right,' she said sulkily.

'I knew you'd come round to my way of thinking in the end,' he murmured in a hatefully self-satisfied tone. 'Car's in the garage. Come on, let's go!'

In silence she went with him and soon they were moving in the moon-silvered darkness over rough ground trodden by cattle during the winter rains. It was just her luck to stumble in one of the deep ruts and a perfectly normal reaction for Kevin to throw an arm around her waist to steady her. Ridiculous of her to feel this stupid shaking—trembling at his touch following tonight's humiliating disclosure of her feelings towards him! He would know that what Andrea had confided to him was the truth. She jerked herself free. She mustn't allow her emotions to show. There must be some way, she thought wildly, in which she could convince him that the story he had been told tonight was far from the truth.

Lost in her thoughts, she stumbled once again and would have fallen headlong had he not once again put a protective arm around her. This time he was holding her close and she wouldn't be able to free herself so easily. At last they moved into the lighted driveway and she managed to slip from his grasp. As a gesture demonstrating her indifference towards him, however, it failed miserably, for he scarcely seemed to notice. 'Luckily we're nearly there,' she murmured shakily. Even to her own ears her laughter had a forced ring.

'Luckily?' She ignored that.

She waited while he got the car from the garage, then climbed into the passenger seat and Kevin got in beside her. For a moment he was silent, looking towards her, an unreadable expression in his eyes.

Christine was unaware of moonlight glimmering on the pale gold of her hair, of softly parted lips and flushed cheeks. She only knew he was gazing in her direction and she braced herself for the blow. Out of the turmoil of her emotions she said defensively, 'What's . . . the matter?'

'Nothing's the matter—now,' he said, and reached a hand towards the starter. They shot down the drive and through the gates and soon they were merging into the stream of vehicles moving along the country road.

Christine had to keep reminding herself of what had happened tonight. Being with him was distracting, she pulled her thoughts together, but if he imagined that because of what Andrea had told him tonight, no doubt with embellishments, she was crazy about him . . .

But you are! said the goblin.

I know, I know, but there's no need for him to know that.

He does know it.

I'll do something about that, she told the devastatingly truthful voice in her mind, and moved as far away from him as possible, which was quite a distance in the big, late-model car. If Kevin noticed her withdrawal, however, he gave no indication.

'Enjoy yourself tonight?'

'Oh yes, yes!' How did one infuse real enthusiasm into one's tone? She did her best to sound sincere.

'That news tonight about Wendy——' She broke off, horrified at her choice of words. 'I mean, getting married in England to Bill and everything,' she stumbled on, 'it was really something!'

'Sure was. She could hardly wait for the Big Announcement to be made. She'll have a heck of a different life from now on. She's got talent, no doubt about that, might even make a name for herself with her paintings over on the other side of the world, and have a lot of fun into the bargain.'

'Yes.'

Christine held her breath. Now was the opportunity for him to let her know of her own blunder to do with Wendy's engagement announcement. To forestall the words she blurted out the first thing that came into her head. 'She might get homesick.'

'Would you,' his voice, deep and soft, was doing things to her resolutions, 'on a honeymoon . . . in Paris?'

She fought for control over her own emotions. 'I'm not Wendy.' With an effort she forced the dangerous subject aside.

'You must think she's really gifted with her painting?'

'I don't think, Christine, I know.' The subject of Wendy's future lasted them all the way back to the house. As Kevin braked to a stop Christine was poised to leap out of the vehicle, but once again she felt his detaining hand as she reached towards the door. If only he wouldn't *touch* her! How could she think of anything else, convince him she didn't care, with her senses in an uproar?

'Wait. I want a word with you.'

She wrenched her hand from his grasp.

'What's the idea, avoiding me all night?' he went on.

'Me? Avoiding you?' The note of surprise she tried to put into her voice emerged as a squeak. 'I don't know how you got that idea.'

'Because it's the truth and you know it!'

The thoughts tumbled through her mind. Did he know or didn't he? If only she could be sure Andrea hadn't confided in him! His voice, deep and compelling, was making her resolves weaken. 'Every time I tried to get near you for a dance——'

'Did you?'

'You know I did.'

She twisted a lock of hair nervously. 'You seemed to

have plenty of partners without me. And Andrea——' She broke off in confusion. Why had she mentioned that of all names to him?

'Andrea?' He sounded genuinely puzzled. Was he pretending to her, letting her off the hook? She stole a sideways glance towards him, but his face was hidden in shadow. 'So that's it!' All at once his voice softened. 'What's Andrea got to do with you and me?'

She decided to play for safety. 'Nothing! Nothing at all! I just thought that maybe——'

'*Christine!*' Something in his voice started the trembling in her once again. She felt his hand on her face, turning her so that she was forced to meet his gaze, then she was submerged in waves of bitter-sweet rapture. Somehow she fought herself back to sanity. Remember he despises you, she thought, he's only trying you out because of having been told tonight that you're crazy about him. All at once she knew what she must do to convince him otherwise. She said thickly, 'Gavin——'

His hand dropped abruptly. 'Are you telling me that you and he——' His voice, she thought bleakly, but with all the tenderness gone from it.

'Why not?' she heard herself say with a laugh that broke on a note of pain. All at once the humiliation and frustrations of the past weeks exploded in anguish and regret. 'Why shouldn't I like him? He doesn't set himself up to judge me, he takes me as I am.'

His voice was very low. 'What about love? You haven't included that in your list of virtues.'

She said in a muffled tone, 'Of course he loves me.'

'I wasn't thinking of him.'

She was silent. All at once the anger died away and suddenly it was very hard to pretend. It must be because of what Kevin had learned tonight that he found her words so hard to believe. It only went to show that he *knew*, even though he hadn't said so in so many words. Well, she had given the lie to Andrea's words. If only it didn't hurt so much!

'I'm asking *you*.' There was something odd in his tone, almost as if it mattered, which was absurd in the circumstances.

'You ask an awful lot of questions,' she threw back at him, and made to open the door of the car. This time he made no attempt to detain her.

CHAPTER NINE

IN the following weeks Wendy's approaching departure helped take Christine's mind from her own insurmountable problems. Involved in the feverish activity of last-minute shopping and packing, trying to keep the array of wedding dress and honeymoon clothing within the limits of air-baggage, Wendy was often on the telephone, begging Christine's advice. The queries were endless regarding the way of life in a far-away Cornish village where her husband-to-be had obtained a practice. 'Do come over today and see me,' Wendy would plead. 'You're the only one in Gisborne who knows all these things.' Then, for perhaps the hundredth time, 'Tell me, is it very different living on the other side of the world?'

'Not once you get past having Christmas in the middle of winter instead of your summertime,' Christine had replied laughingly. 'And in Cornwall . . . you know something? You might be pleasantly surprised to find you feel quite at home there. It's so picturesque—blue sea, harbour and boats, and what do you know, there are tree ferns growing there the same as you have here, and lots of flowers you have here. Truly!'

'Really? Oh, thanks a lot, Christine, I feel I love the place already. I'm all packed now, just ready and waiting.' The high excited tones ran on with scarcely a pause. 'You will come to the airport to see me off?'

'I'll be there.'

On the following evening when she went with Laurie and Jan to the airport they found a crowd already gathered in the departure lounge. Everyone for miles around appeared to have come to the airport to farewell the local girl who was leaving on the first lap of her long journey to the other side of the world. A buzz of talk and laughter echoed around the big room as Wendy, looking trim and attractive in her linen slack suit, found herself, for the second time in a month, the centre of attention.

'Christine!' At sight of the new arrivals Wendy made her way through the throng. Flushed and laughing, she caught Christine's arm. 'There! I'm going to make you stick close until the last minute!' Almost immediately a group pushed between them and over the heads of strangers Christine caught Wendy's piercing tones. 'You will come to see me—us, I mean, Bill and me, in Cornwall next month, won't you, Christine? You promised! You have got the address I gave you?'

Christine called back, 'Don't worry, it's all written down in my notebook.'

'Just imagine,' Wendy managed to get back to Christine's side, 'you'll be our first visitor from home, my best friend——'

'Hey there, Wendy!' A group of newcomers crowded between them. 'Just came to wish you all the best for the trip!' Gifts were pressed on the excited girl and in the confusion Christine found herself once more forced back among the milling throng. At the same time she was aware of an oh-so-familiar masculine figure making his way purposefully in her direction. The next minute she looked up to meet Kevin's unsmiling gaze.

'Is that right?' he demanded tersely.

'Is what right?'

She knew exactly what he meant, but she was playing for time.

'Don't play about, Christine,' the deep tones seemed to her to be oddly charged with emotion, 'you know what I'm getting at! Your taking off again for home so soon!'

I'm only waiting now because of you. Aloud she said in a low tone, 'I never intended to stay . . . all that long.'

She saw a muscle jerk in his cheek. 'I get it.' His voice was terse. 'With a good manager on the place like Laurie——'

Laurie, her 'manager'. She could have laughed aloud, only it wasn't really funny, only desperately sad.

In the rising echo of sound around them she had to strain to catch his words, 'You and Gavin, I take it?'

At that moment a voice on the loudspeaker cut across the uproar. 'Now boarding, Flight Number 4415 . . . Now boarding . . .' The crowd surged between them and Christine found herself carried along with the crowd towards the barrier. At that moment, clear and pure above the hubbub, rose the sound of Maori voices in the traditional song of farewell. Everyone joined in the haunting refrain, the voices surging out through the open doors and into the clear air beyond.

> 'Now is the hour
> For me to say goodbye,
> Soon I'll be sailing
> Far across the sea.
> When I am gone will you
> Remember me?'

Christine stood waving with the others to the girl who was limping across the tarmac towards the plane set against a backdrop of darkening hills. There was a lump in Christine's throat, but whether the ache of sadness was for Wendy or because of her own imminent departure she couldn't have said.

Presently the plane lifted with a roar that faded into the distance and still the crowd lined the barrier rails, waving and watching until the plane was no more than a smudge against the clear lemon afterglow in a sunset sky. At last, as well-wishers dispersed, Christine turned and made her way back through the lounge and into the car park.

During the following two weeks—she knew there were two because she was counting the days—she didn't see Kevin. In all fairness she had to admit that he was scarcely likely to make any attempt to see her now that she had gone to such pains to pinpoint how little desire she had for his company, while dancing or otherwise. Funny, she mused wryly, that introducing Gavin's name as an excuse for avoiding him at Wendy's party was the truth, in an upside-down sort of way. She supposed that deep down somewhere she had known all along that Gavin cared for her a lot. Nowadays he needed no excuse for his frequent visits to Glendene and even though he hadn't put his feelings in so many words she couldn't help but be aware of his growing love for her. It showed in the tone of his voice, the way he looked at her. If she could tell, probably others could too. No wonder she so often intercepted Ella's speculative glance roving from herself to the bearded young man. Or that Jan was becoming more relaxed in her dealings with her and had only occasionally the flashes of jealousy that for so long had marred their friendship.

As the slow days dragged by Christine spent most of her time out of doors. Most mornings she was out early saddling up Brownie in readiness for helping Laurie shift steers to different pastures or to ride around the boundary fences, anything to take her mind, if only temporarily, from Kevin. Not that anything could achieve that miracle, but work helped. If only there weren't the long nights to get through!

Then one morning the lawyer's letter arrived from town. Christine's hands were not quite steady as she slit the envelope and ran her eyes down the legal document transferring her property and stock to Laurie. Now there was no longer anything to keep her here. Only one piece of unfinished business remained, and that was to acquaint Kevin with the truth. It was funny, though, now that the moment for which she had waited so long was actually here and she was free at last to vindicate herself, a curious reluctance held her back. Could it be because at the back of her mind the thought persisted, would he be all that interested in her affairs? No matter, he had to know. To go on living at Glendene the way she was now, just waiting, just hoping, was to give way to wishful thinking. Better tell Kevin what must be said, book a flight back to London and try somehow to begin a new life for herself—difficult to do when every instinct pulled her back here, but she must force herself to be strong, and just to prove it she would get the car from the garage this minute. She would drive into town and book herself on a plane for England.

All the way to town and back she tried to think of some way in which she could see Kevin alone. In the state of turmoil she was in it was an effort not to surrender to the longing to drive right on to his home now, this minute, but some remnants of common sense prevailed. She would need to have some excuse for dropping in on the man and maybe if she waited a little while an opportunity might arise to put her plan into action. She garaged the car and had scarcely entered the house when Laurie coming into the kitchen at that moment handed her the chance she wanted. She could scarcely believe his words. 'Feel like a run up to Kevin's place? They're hunting over his property today. Thought we might take a run up there and have a look-see.'

'What's that about a run out?' Jan, coming into the room, glanced from Laurie to Christine. 'Because if there's anything on I'm going to be in on it too.'

'Why not?' Laurie told her. 'I was going to ring you, but you've saved me the trouble.'

Christine saw some of the tension and suspicion in Jan's eyes die away. She wants to believe there's nothing that matters between Laurie and me, that it's Gavin I'm interested in, her thoughts ram. Most of the time she does believe it. If only she would let herself she'd like me, but just sometimes, like now, that jealous nature of hers gets the better of her. Oh well, it won't be for long now. Soon everyone will be happy, except me.

She stuffed her precious letter in the pocket of her blue

jeans and soon she was climbing into the car with the other two. Laurie and Jan, involved in their own concerns, kept up a constant flow of talk and laughter and appeared unaware of Christine's silence. Deep down she knew that even though she now had a genuine excuse for coming to Kevin's home, she was at the stage of love where she had to see him and would have leaped at any opportunity just to look at him. She despised herself for the weakness, but that didn't mean she could help herself.

When they reached the driveway of the big house they could see that trestle tables had been set up below the long verandah and Andrea was busy setting out cups and saucers she was taking from a cardboard carton.

Some of the consternation she felt must have shown in her expression, because Jan said laughingly, 'Don't look so surprised. Mrs Hawke hasn't died or anything, just taken off for one of her little shopping jaunts to town.' She added as if it were of no particular importance, 'Kevin must have asked her to be hostess for him today.'

'That figures,' Laurie observed with a grin.

It figured only too well. Christine's heart plunged. Why was it that knowing Kevin was not for her, she still couldn't bear any other girl to be important to him? So important that before long she would take on for real the role she was playing today. And to think she had imagined Mrs Hawke's veiled remark regarding a girl her son was becoming interested in to mean Wendy, whereas of course the older woman had been referring to Andrea. Andrea, who was so eminently suitable to share his life with her sheep-station background, her show-jumping experience.

'Hi, Andrea!' Laurie's call brought her back to the present. He had slowed the car to a pause on the driveway. 'You're not riding today?'

'Not today.' Christine wondered if it were her imagination, or did the other girl look more confident than ever? 'Hi, you two.' Andrea's gaze rested on Christine's face. 'Kevin wanted me to act hostess for him today, so I told him I didn't mind giving up the hunt for one day.'

I'll bet you didn't, Christine's heart observed.

'If you're thinking of going after them,' Andrea was saying in her bright assertive way, 'they went up the hill that-away,' she indicated a nearby green slope, 'but that was over an hour ago. Goodness knows where they are by now.'

'We'll find them,' Laurie said, and put his hand to the starter.

'See you later,' Andrea called happily, and went on with her task.

They took the winding track up the hill, but even when they reached the summit they could see no red coats or hounds or horses. 'Probably out of sight down on the flats,' Laurie commented, and turned back the way they had come. The sound of a horn carried faintly on the breeze guided them up another slope and they were half way up the steep track when they came in sight of huntsman, hounds and riders on a grassy patch between the hills. Christine, however, had eyes for only one rider, the man seated on Trooper. Her horse, her man, and she had lost them both. Or had she ever meant anything to Kevin? Those rare moments of tenderness, the changed look she had surprised on his face at times, almost as if he didn't want to love her or even like her but something stronger than his will drew him to her. She pulled her thoughts together. Now you're being fanciful, she scolded herself.

The next moment the riders were off, following the pack up a slope, clearing one after another the barbed wire fences strung at angles across the hills. Christine watched as Kevin put Trooper to a high fence and horse and rider sailed over with inches to spare. She didn't even hold her breath as she watched, for she knew he would think nothing of the jump. They were two of a kind, the rider and his mount, fearless, dependable—and *damnedly stubborn once they got an idea in their heads!*

Laurie had started the car and was about to climb higher for a better view of the riders below when Christine on an impulse decided not to go further with the other two. 'I'll follow on foot,' she told them.

'Are you sure?' Jan was trying to hide the note of relief in her voice.

Laurie said: 'Want me to come back this way and pick you up later?'

She shook her head, her gaze moving towards the vehicles turning into the track below. 'Don't trouble, there are sure to be some cars on the road and someone will give me a lift back to the house.' Privately she had no intention of joining the crowd that later would be gathered around the trestle tables, but there was no need for Laurie to know that.

'Okay, then.'

Left alone, Christine began to climb the hillside, a solitary figure on the dusty winding trail worn by countless sheep over the years.

At the summit the wind blew fresh and cool on her hot face and she sank down in the long dry grass. The peaks rising all around her dwarfed her own sense of heartbreak and frustration. For the sight of Andrea acting as hostess in Kevin's home had shaken her. There was no hope of seeing Kevin alone today, she mused bleakly. She must have been crazy even to have considered such a thing. It would be difficult enough on a hunt day under ordinary circumstances to see Kevin alone, but now, with Andrea presiding over the refreshment tables, she could scarcely arrive at the house uninvited. No, it would have to be another day. After all, she tried to rally her sinking spirits, one day couldn't make much difference. Only somehow it did.

The buzz of insects in the grass, the hot sun on her face combined to lull the pain in her heart. She hadn't intended to love him, but love had come unbidden and life would never be the same again. She leaned back, remembering. So soon now she would be leaving here for ever, returning to England alone. Even the black fear in her mind about the high jump was still there, strong and implacable as ever. She had never succeeded in getting the better of that particular enemy. What had she been hoping for, miracles? That Kevin would one day come to love her as she loved him? That she would clear the high jumps as fearlessly as ever? *Some hope!*

Suddenly she felt strong masculine hands covering her eyes and a voice from behind her said triumphantly, 'Guess who?'

'Gavin!' She struggled free. 'Where on earth did you spring from?'

Laughing, he dropped down beside her. 'Well, I didn't come to see the hunt, if that's what you're thinking. I had something much more important in mind—tracking you! Quite a trail you led me, my girl. Ella told me you'd come up here with Laurie and Jan and when I met up with them they reported having dropped you off half way down the hill and said you were following the hunt on foot. So I slogged along on foot too for a while, then I began to use my brains, borrowed a guy's binocs and spotted you going for your life up here!'

'I wasn't!' She sat up indignantly. 'I was just walk-ing——'

'Only as if you had half the hunt after you. You don't really get much of a sight of them from up here.' He peered towards the gully below where an odd black jacket was visible. 'But then does it matter?' He leaned back, his face to the sun, chewing a long stem of grass reflectively. 'Mmm, nice spot you've got here. Private too. If you want to get away from it all, that suits me.' His twinkling gaze took in Christine's tousled fair hair, the sun-kissed hollow above the V of her cotton blouse. 'You're getting a fantastic tan these last few weeks. Life out here suits you—Chris-tine,' all at once his low tones throbbed with passion, 'I hadn't meant to say anything so soon, but . . .' He caught her roughly to him, burying his face in her hair.

To save him the embarrassment of what she knew was coming she shook her head free. 'It's no use,' she told him gently.

He raised an anguished face. 'You can't make me believe that! We've only just go to know each other. Give me a bit of time and——'

She shook her head. 'That's just what we haven't got.'
Better to make a clean cut and get it over with. 'You may
as well know—I went to town this morning and booked my
seat on a plane for England.'

He stared back at her, his eyes dazed and disbelieving.
'You did—what?' Christine hated herself for having dealt
him the blow. 'You couldn't, you wouldn't ... we were getting along so well.'

'I know, I know, but getting along together isn't enough.'

'It's enough for me! It's a start!' If only she had realised
how deep were his feelings for her. She had known he liked
her a lot of course, but this——

'Economy fare!' he cried with a flash of his old lighthearted manner. 'Book three weeks ahead and save your
money? Am I right?'

'You're right.'

'Then that means I've got twenty-one days to bring you
around to my way of thinking. And I warn you, I'm never
going to give up, not until I see another man's ring on your
finger. We're right for each other. Don't you see,' the eager
words fell fast from his lips, 'we like the same things,
laugh at the same stupid jokes, like ones I make. We'd
make a great team, you and me, a man and woman team.
Come on, love,' he was covering her face and neck with
kisses, 'a chance, that's all I'm asking you. Tell me I've got
a chance?'

She said in a low tone, 'I wish I could.'

Something in her voice must have got through to him at
last, because he let her go. 'You really mean it?' The next
moment the despairing note in his voice fled as his opti-
mistic nature asserted itself. 'Now, I mean, but I'll *make*
you care——'

'I do care for you as a friend. You've been wonderful to
me ever since we met.'

He said on a sigh, 'As a friend.' Then with his old merry
smile, 'I guess that's a start.' Christine could scarcely catch
the low tones that were charged with feeling. 'Tell me just

one thing, there's no one else? No other guy who's mad about you.'

'No one.' And that, she thought with irony, is only too true.

Gavin heaved a sigh of relief. 'Well, that's something, a big advantage to me.'

'It's no use,' she said quietly. 'Don't you see, your hoping and all that that I'll change my mind—it's just no use.'

'That's what you think! Christine,' he clasped her hands in his eager grasp, his pleading tones making her feel more than ever regretful that she had nothing to offer him, not even hope. 'We could have a terrific life together here. You know you like it out here in Kiwi-land. You settled down here as if you'd known it all your life.'

She smiled and in an attempt to lighten the emotional atmosphere said wryly, 'You didn't see me that first day when I was at Glendene all by myself except for young Patrick and I had to rely on him for advice. It was a nightmare. I'd have hopped a plane for home right away, if I'd had the chance.'

'But you are going back? You're leaving Laurie in charge, is that it?'

She hesitated. 'Something like that.'

'*Why*, Christine?'

It was the question to which she had no answer, except the truth. 'I——' her voice faltered away.

Gavin misinterpreted her silence. 'There you are, you haven't got any special reason—and let me tell you, my girl, you've got a very special reason, namely me, for staying on, and on and on. I'm not very good at this,' he muttered indistinctly, 'never thought I could care for any girl, not this way. Just a hope,' he pleaded, 'that's all I'm asking.' Then seeing the expression of her face, 'No? In that case I'll change my tactics. It's a good beach day and the tide's full in at Wainui.' He added persuasively, 'It's a nice run too.'

'Oh yes!—Let's do that!' He must, she thought the next

minute, have been surprised at the warmth of her answer.

'Right! We'll drop in at your place on the way and pick up your swimming gear, have a barbecue tea on the beach.'

'Love to!' For a girl who had apparently come here for the special purpose of following the hunt he must, she thought, be rather surprised at the relief in her voice. Actually the offer was just what she wanted, a chance to escape, for the prospect of being forced to join the riders and onlookers at the end of the day's hunt was something she couldn't face. The very fact of her being here at all was bad enough, it would no doubt lend credence to all that Andrea had told Kevin, if she had told him, about Christine's feelings for him. The thought of being at the receiving end of Andrea's condescending hospitality was more than she could bear, why not admit it?

She became aware that Gavin had got to his feet and was grinning down at her. She tried not to see the shadow of pain in his eyes.

'There you are! You're proving my point already. A start, you said? How about a kiss to seal the bargain?'

He bent towards her, but Christine had sprung to her feet, pulling grass and twigs from her hair.

'Okay, I can wait. You know something? I really thought you were keen to see the hunt——'

She smiled up at him. 'I'd rather see you—and the local scenery,' she added hastily at the expression in his eyes. Goodness, she would need to be careful in her choice of words if she weren't to raise false hopes. She of all people should know the misery that could lead to. 'You won't say any more about——'

His eyes dwelt on her with a tenderness that cut her to the heart. 'About marrying you, you mean? I won't say anything, I'll just keep working on it!' His grin lacked a little of its lustre as he took her hand in his. 'Come on, down the track with you, woman! Your carriage awaits!'

Together they ran down the steep grassy slope, to arrive breathlessly on the pathway where the grey van was parked. As they moved forward, Gavin's appreciative

glance swept the peaks rising around them and Christine
was relieved that he was apparently content to drop the
dangerous subject of marriage, at least for the time being.
But the matter would be on his mind just the same, she
knew. Oh, didn't she know!

'Nice country this,' he was saying. 'It's taken a few
generations of the Hawke clan to bring it all into cultiva-
tion. Now of course Kevin's the lucky guy who's reaping
the benefit of the hard work of the pioneers. In those early
days when the country was first settled it was a matter of
hard slog with none of the help of modern machinery. Oh
well, that's the way it goes—there he is now!' They were
dropping down towards the flats to come in sight of a
group of riders who were taking their mounts over a high
barbed fence. Christine, however, had eyes only for Kevin
and watched as he and his mount took the jump effortlessly to land lightly on the other side.

'You're not listening to a word I've been saying. Too
fascinated by the man himself?'

A random shot? She couldn't tell. Groping in her mind,
she came up with some sort of answer. 'It's Trooper. That's
why I came over here today,' she went on in a rush of
words. 'I thought—hoped Kevin might be taking him out
and I wanted to see if he gave a good account of himself.'

'Who? Kevin—or Trooper?'

'Trooper, of course.' She turned her face aside, hoping
he hadn't noticed the flags of tell-tale colour that had risen
in her cheeks.

'Couldn't blame you if you did fall for the guy.' He didn't
guess at the truth, thank heaven, or he wouldn't be speaking so lightly. 'I mean, Kevin's got it made, every single
thing a man could want. The owner of a terrific sheep
station, one of the best in the country, with horses to hunt
every day of the week. A girl who's mad about him, anyone
can see that——'

'Mad about him?' The expression of shock and anguish
in her face, her wide startled eyes would have given her

away, but Gavin's gaze was on the hounds disappearing over a low rise.

'Don't tell me you haven't noticed the way Andrea follows him around like a puppy? All nice and matey if you like, but all the same she's always there, she can't let him out of her sight. And if that's not love——' He sent her a rueful smile. 'Look who's talking! I mean, you only have to see the state I'm in at the moment, and it's all your fault!'

Christine said, 'They've been brought up to the same way of life, like the same things. According to Ella it's always been that way.' Who was she trying to convince, Gavin or herself? 'Anyway,' she couldn't seem to banish the thought of Andrea and Kevin from her mind, 'she's not riding with him today. She's busy acting hostess at the house while Mrs Hawke's away.'

'I told you!' Gavin cried triumphantly. 'Good old Andrea. She's working on the infiltration policy—today the front steps, tomorrow the whole house! She might make it yet. It won't be for want of trying if she doesn't. For my money I'd say there's only one thing that can stop her now, and that is if the guy happened to meet someone new and the old chemistry started working.'

Christine didn't dare glance his way. Was he merely idly talking, or did he guess that that chemistry was already working its devastating magic between herself and Kevin and had done so from the first moment of their meeting? Deny it, ignore it, they couldn't escape its power.

'You don't agree?'

She became aware of his glance.

'Oh yes, yes,' she said in some confusion.

His smile was touched with wry amusement. 'You mean you wouldn't know? It's all right, I'm not going to go on and on about,' his eyes softened, 'my own lovely, lovely problem.' He started the car and they moved in the direction of the winding drive. 'You did say you wanted a swim?'

She nodded. 'I can hardly wait.'

'Right!' They hurtled down the slope. 'Wainui coming up!'

CHAPTER TEN

THAT evening when Gavin brought her back to the house Christine told Ella and Fred of her impending departure. She was surprised and more than a little touched by the reaction her news evoked, for in spite of Ella's initial dislike and suspicion towards her there was no doubt that they would be sorry to see her go.

Fred passed a hand over his sparse locks in a puzzled gesture, his lined face registering both shock and dismay. 'We're sorry to hear that. It's bad news for Ella and me, and that's the truth! We've got used to your being here with us and having someone young and pretty around the place has meant a lot to both of us. We thought maybe you felt the same way about us.'

All Christine could do was to murmur inadequately, 'I know, I know. It's been wonderful for me being here with you but . . .' Her voice trailed away.

Ella's sharp eyes were taking in Christine's discomfiture. 'I can't imagine,' she said flatly, 'why you're taking off like this all of a sudden—Gavin,' she appealed to the man perched on the edge of Christine's chair, 'can't you do something about keeping her here?'

'Don't look at me!' Christine realised he had himself well in hand. 'I've been arguing with her all afternoon trying to make her change her mind.' And to Christine, 'How about making it just a month or so longer? You can see how we're all going to miss you.'

She said in a muffled tone, 'It would be just the same then.'

Laurie said cheerfully, 'Oh well, if she's made up her mind to go.' His gaze rested on her downcast face and she could guess at the thoughts that were passing through his mind. Is the land transfer all fixed up, then? Is that why she's suddenly booked her air flight back to England?

It wasn't, however, until later in the evening when Gavin had gone back to town and Ella and Fred were absorbed in their favourite television programme that Laurie was able to put to Christine the question that trembled on his lips.

She was flicking the pages of a women's magazine without taking in the contents of the articles when he paused at her side to say in a low tone, 'Why the sudden take-off?'

She raised her heavy-lidded gaze. 'Just that the lawyer's letter came through today in the mail. Everything's arranged as we planned. No loose ends now ... except me. I guess,' she added on a sigh, 'that it's time I went back now that things are all straightened out here.'

'Pity,' there was a note of genuine regret in his voice. 'Jan and I were counting on your being here for our wedding. It's only another six months to wait.'

She shook her head. 'I'm sorry.'

'We're sorry too. And how about Gavin? You're not planning to leave the guy pining here for you, are you?'

'I can't help that,' she said in a low distressed tone. Half to herself she murmured, 'I didn't ask him to go overboard for me. It ... just happened.'

'It generally does,' Laurie observed drily. All at once his voice changed to a crisper note, almost a tone of authority. 'Christine, I owe you everything. Is it any use my trying to say Thank you——'

'You don't need to. It was never mine, all this, anyway—and I'm sure you'll be a much better landowner than I could ever be. There's one thing you could do for me,' her tone changed to a note of urgency, 'don't say anything about all this to anyone else, not until I let you know—do you mind?'

'Whatever you say, not a word, Scout's honour, cross my heart, until you give me the signal.' A slow smile spread over his face. 'Can't you just see Jan's face when I let her in on this news! And old Fred. He'll like you more than ever. Ella will go around telling everyone she knew all the

time that this would happen. She's always wise after the
event—look, we'll have to give you a send-off——'

'No, *please*!' The thought of the gathering of friends and
well-wishers was something she couldn't face, not the way
she felt about leaving here. 'I don't want any fuss, I'll just
slip away——'

'Nuts to that! Everyone will want to come and wish you
a good trip back. You can't do them out of it. The old
hotel,' Laurie ran on, taking for granted her acceptance of
the plan, 'It's a wreck and a ruin, but I guess it will stand
up for one more night. Kind of fitting, wouldn't you say,
the first place you hit on that night you arrived here——'

'You said it was to be burned down?'

'True, true,' he waved her objection aside, 'but we never
ever got around to putting a match to it.' Suddenly he was
no longer shy and gauche but gay, self-confident. 'We'll
give it a grand send-off too!'

What could she say? He seemed determined to make the
farewell gesture and she knew that if he didn't, others
would arrange a function on her behalf. It would mean she
would have to pretend for a little longer, that was all. *And
see Kevin for one last time*, her heart added.

Once the others in the house were convinced that her
mind was made up they ceased to try to persuade her to
stay and instead they concentrated on the farewell dance
to be held on the night before her departure for England.
Christine was only vaguely aware of the planning that was
going on around her. Her thoughts were elsewhere. Kevin
. . . the way in which news travelled on the grapevine in the
country districts, he must have heard of her intended departure from here by now. Each time the phone rang she
leaped to answer it. Goodness knows why, she would tell
herself the next moment, for there was no reason why he
should contact her to say goodbye. He would know too
about the farewell function being arranged on her behalf
and that would be good enough for him. A face in the
crowd, that was all she would mean to him on that night.

All the time at the back of her mind there burned the

question; how to see him, tell him what he must be told, without making a fool of herself? There must be some innocent-seeming way to work in a visit to Mata-Rangi if only she could think of it. And still as the days fled by, no feasible plan presented itself. One difficulty in the way was that Gavin had taken to coming to the house daily, even if the visit was a short one. His grey van was a familiar sight in the driveway. 'Just dropped in when I was passing this way to see how you were!' But the shadowed eyes belied the light words. 'I mean, a few minutes are better than nothing!' Love made one very perceptive, didn't she know it, and what if he guessed her secret?

She was aware of Ella too, ever-watchful and clearly puzzled over Christine's apathetic attitude, the lack of appetite she tried so hard to hide. To take off for Mata-Rangi without some sort of excuse would be sufficient to make those sharp eyes put two and two together and come up with the shame-making answer. 'She's mad about him, simply can't keep away from him!' No, she would have to do better than that!

In the end the opportunity she longed for came out of the blue. 'A telephone call for you from Hawkes' place.' Ella was holding the receiver towards Christine.

'Oh!' It was difficult to conceal anything from Ella's gaze, especially when her heart was behaving so oddly. She suppressed the urge to snatch the receiver from Ella's hand and made her tone light and casual. 'Yes?'

'Oh, Christine——' it was Mrs Hawke's voice at the other end of the line and Christine's spirits did a nose-dive. 'I've just heard the news about you leaving us. I'm so sorry you have to go so soon, quite a shock to us all really. There's no bad news at home, I hope? Your mother——'

'No, no, nothing like that.' Did you but know, dear lady, the bad news is right here in this little township and your son is the cause of it. 'But I have to go.' Idiot, why hadn't she taken the trouble to invent some plausible explanation for her sudden return to England? Now her mind seemed to have gone completely blank.

'I suppose,' Mrs Hawke was saying in her pleasant tones, 'that we'll just have to make the best of it. I know you'll be frightfully busy just now with your packing and so on, but I would like you to come up and see me. Just a chat and a look around the garden—the oleanders are at their best just now. I don't suppose that today——'

Christine forgot all about being discreet and broke in eagerly, 'Oh *yes*! Today would be fine! I'd love to come!' Belatedly she added, 'I'm not all that busy, not yet.'

'That's good news. I'll look forward to seeing you, then. Sorry I can't send someone over to pick you up and bring you here, but all the men are away. Some of them are taking part in the events in the rodeo today that's being held up the coast and Kevin has given them all the day off.'

Had Kevin too gone to the rodeo? Christine would have to take a chance on that.

'Oh, I've got the car, thank you.' As she hung up the receiver she breathed a silent Thank you, Mrs Hawke. You'll never know what your invitation means to me today. At least, I hope you'll never know.

All the way as she made the journey to Mata-Rangi Christine was conscious of the crackle of paper in the pocket of her jeans. She couldn't wait to reach her destination and unconsciously she pressed her foot down on the accelerator. She shot forward, moving down the hill at speed, then she was driving along the flats. More than one passing motorist looked back in surprise at the girl with the set pale face who was staring straight ahead, not recognising anyone in any passing vehicle. Odd behaviour on the part of a girl who was considered to be one of the most careful drivers in the district. Christine didn't even see the other drivers on the road. Today she had but one thought in her mind. Fortunately when she reached the turn-off leading to the station among the hills there were no wandering steers or vagrant sheep to contend with on the road, and still travelling at speed, she swung around bends with a scream of brakes. Why not, when she had the road to herself?

Don't look at the homestead from this spot on the way, she told herself. Don't remind yourself of the day when Kevin had stopped the car specially to point out his home up above. Probably he followed the same procedure with every girl he took to the homestead for the first time. No need for all that with Andrea. To her Mata-Rangi was already 'home'—well, practically. She hurtled around a bend and loose stones flew up to hit the undercarriage of the vehicle. Why torture herself with memories? Better to get it all over with, then perhaps she would at last be able to forget this brief New Zealand interlude. Still without slackening speed she sped up the driveway to pull up at the verandah steps. On the last occasion when she had visited here Andrea had been presiding over the refreshment tables. A preview for the future? Lucky Andrea.

She was hurrying up the steps when Mrs Hawke came out on the verandah to meet her. The older woman drew her inside, chatting warmly while she served tea and freshly-baked scones, but all the time Christine was aware even in her own turmoil of spirit that something was troubling the other woman. It showed in her listening attitude as though she were expecting someone to join them at any moment as well as in a lack of interest in what Christine was saying. Clearly Mrs Hawke's thoughts were elsewhere. On another level, however, Christine's mind was busy thinking and planning, absorbed in her own affairs. It would have been too much to have hoped for that Kevin would be at the house this afternoon. On that earlier occasion when she had come here he had seemed so anxious to show her around the property—but don't forget, she reminded herself bleakly, that at that time you hadn't made it so plain to him that you didn't wish to speak to him or see him ever again. Besides, on that day he was in the market for Trooper.

As they strolled around the flower borders and Mrs Hawke indicated the various blooms, the late roses, the showers of pink and white and red oleander blossoms, the impression of strain deepened until at last Christine said impulsively, 'Forgive me for saying this, but there's nothing wrong, is there, Mrs Hawke? I mean, if there is just tell me and I'll come some other time. I've still got a few days left free yet, you know.'

'Oh, it's nothing to do with you, my dear,' the older woman appeared to find some relief in confiding her problem. 'It's just that Kevin——'

'Kevin!' A knife plunged deep into Christine's heart. 'He's all right, isn't he?' she cried in alarm.

'I only hope so, but to tell you the truth I'm worried sick about him. Stupid and silly of me to feel like this. After living all these years in the country I should be used to the men being a bit overdue when they go out on a tractor to work in the back paddocks, but I can't help being concerned. It's just not like him not to get back on time when he said he would, especially when he knew you were coming today.'

Christine was very still. 'He knew about me, then?'

'My dear, that's what's driving me crazy. He said he'd be back by lunch time. He wanted to be sure to have time to scrub up before you came, he told me. I know he wouldn't have missed seeing you, that nothing would have stopped him except . . .' Her voice trailed anxiously away and the colour left her face. After a moment she went on, 'He had a job to do down in the gully—clearing a ditch, but he said it wouldn't take him long and he'd be back in good time so as to be here when you arrived.' She glanced at her wrist-watch and when she looked up Christine took in the lines of strain around her mouth. 'That was hours ago. I keep telling myself that the tractor has broken down, only,' she gave a hollow laugh, 'it happens to be brand new.'

She bit her lip distractedly. 'I suppose what's on my mind all the time is the accident that happened to my own father when I was a girl living on a station not far from here. He didn't ever come home again, and when one of the shepherds went to find out what was keeping him he found

Dad pinned beneath his overturned tractor. He'd been killed instantly.' She made an effort to pull herself together. 'But all that was a long time ago. It's quite absurd of me to think the worst has happened just because Kevin is late getting home today. If only it hadn't happened today when the rodeo is on up the coast and all the men are away! Kevin has gone to ride in the rodeo every other year, but when he heard you were coming ... now there's no one here to send out to look for him. I can't help thinking,' her voice broke, 'that if there's been an accident he could be lying out in the hills somewhere helpless and alone. And with all the men away at the rodeo ... I think I'll ring a friend who lives on the main road,' she suggested worriedly, 'there must be some men around today.'

'No!' Christine sprang forward. 'Don't ring anyone, Mrs Hawke. I'll go and look for him. Just tell me which way to go.'

'But you couldn't possibly ... there's no road, just the sheep tracks over the hills.'

'I'll ride! If you'll help me to saddle up one of the horses?'

Mrs Hawke looked doubtful. 'I know you mean well, but you're like me, from what I hear, not a very experienced rider. I can't have you an accident case and Kevin walking in afterwards as good as new.' She smiled a wavering smile. 'He would never forgive me.'

'I can ride well enough, when I have to.' Christine spoke out of a newly-found sense of confidence.

'It'll take you ages, opening and shutting all those gates. It's some miles away, the back boundary.' Then seeing Christine's mind was made up, 'Come with me and we'll saddle up one of the stock ponies.'

'If I'm going I've got to get there quickly.' Christine's thoughts were clear as crystal, all doubts fled from her mind. 'I'll take Trooper, he won't waste any time.'

'Trooper?' For a moment Mrs Hawke forgot to be apprehensive and looked merely flabbergasted.

'Yes, yes,' Christine's voice was impatient. 'Don't worry,

I can handle him. I used to be a show-jumper once.'

'At least he's handy,' Mrs Hawke said faintly. 'Kevin was riding Trooper this morning and he left him in a paddock by the house.'

'Let's go, then!' They hurried towards the harness shed and Mrs Hawke took down a saddle from its bracket.

'This is the one Kevin uses for Trooper. Here's the bridle and the sheepskin.' The two women went up the slope together.

To her relief Christine found that the grey thoroughbred showed no objection to being caught and saddled, even by a girl whose fingers were shaking uncontrollably as she fitted the bit into the horse's mouth. But the trembling was due to haste and had nothing to do with fear. Today her mind was too occupied with the urgency of her mission to leave room for any other emotion. An image of an upturned tractor, a man pinned beneath it, hovered at the back of her mind. She tried to put the picture aside, but it returned to haunt her. It happened so often, didn't it? One read in the papers of countless accidents of that kind in these country districts. And if anything dreadful had happened to Kevin, Kevin who had wanted to be at home when she called, even if only to say goodbye ... Let me be in time, she prayed. Let him not be hurt—or worse. I'll never ask for anything else, not even his love, but please, *please* make him not be hurt.

She tightened the girth and gathering up the reins, leaped into the saddle. Mrs Hawke flung open the gate to the paddock. 'You know the way? Straight on over the hill, then up the next hill, the one with the line of pines, then down the other side into the gully.' She managed a wavering smile. 'You'll probably meet up with him on the way, but if you don't——' Suddenly her voice broke. 'Hurry, Christine! Hurry!'

'Trust me!' A backward glance, an encouraging wave and she was away! The big grey, as if sensing the urgency of their mission, needed no encouragement but took off at a lively pace and soon they were climbing the sheep-dotted hillside. Half way up the slope Christine caught sight of a barbed wire fence looming ahead. There would be a gate somewhere along the fence, but she had no intention of wasting time searching for an opening. Seemingly her mount was of the same mind, for as she set Trooper to the wire he gathered himself, spread out and sailed over to land safely on the opposite side. An encouraging pat and they were off again at a fast canter, moving over the summit of the hill and down the incline, while sheep scattered in panic at their approach. Another hill, boundary fences looming up to be safely negotiated and left behind. What matter that Trooper was a horse with a hard mouth? Who wanted to pull him up anyway? Not her, not today, when time was all that mattered. Time—and something else. At last Christine faced the thought that had appeared to age Kevin's mother in the space of a few hours—finding him alive!

At last she came in sight of the boundary line of pines and urged Trooper to an even faster pace on the narrow sheep track. They hurtled over the top of the hill and now they were going down on the opposite side. A fence barred the way and she set her mount to it almost automatically. Then as she rode on down the slope in the direction of the bush-filled gully below, her heart gave a great leap, for a tractor was tilted on its side and a man appeared to be pinned between it and the bank of the ditch. That spot of colour ... please God, make it just the colour of his shirt and not blood. As she came nearer she realised that that prayer at least had been answered. Reaching the ditch at last, she pulled Trooper to a halt, then leaped from the saddle and ran towards him. Breathlessly the words tumbled from her lips. 'Darling, darling, you're not hurt? You're all right?'

The next moment she realised he was securely pinned between tractor and the crumbling bank, a tyre pressed hard against his leg. For a man who she had feared might well be dead he looked surprisingly alive, even from behind the barricade of his tilted tractor.

'Nothing's wrong with me! I'm just mad!' All at once his tone softened. 'Though I don't mind telling you I'm feeling better every minute now that you've arrived—why didn't you let on to me you could ride so well?'

'Never mind about that. I'll tell you all about it later.' In her relief at finding him unhurt had her emotions tricked her into betraying herself by calling him 'darling'? she wondered. If only she could remember! 'You're the one who's in trouble right now.' She peered forward. 'Is there any use in my trying to shift it?'

'Sweetheart, you wouldn't have a hope in hell!' *Sweetheart*. Her pulses leaped. 'Tell you what you can do, though. See the heap of fence posts over there? How about bringing one here?'

She sped away to return with a post she had picked up from among the heap lying in the dried grass.

'Good girl! Now if you could shove it between the tractor and the bank it would be a load off my mind. The way things are right now, each time I have a go at shifting the tractor the darn thing flips a bit nearer my way. If it moves too far I've had it, so when I saw you coming hell for leather over the hill I decided not to take any more risks.'

'Thank heaven for that!' She was pushing the post between the tractor and the bank. 'There! Will that do?'

'You've done wonders. Just wait until I get free and I'll thank you properly.'

Suddenly she found it difficult to meet his bright, alive gaze. 'What . . . happened?'

'Just a spot of bad luck, actually. I was driving the tractor along the edge of the bank when the ground caved in and the tractor slipped sideways into the ditch. I did my best to get it out, but no way, every time it slid a bit further until it got me securely jammed between the tyre and the bank. It was a bit risky to try and move it any more. I can tell you that seeing you heading over the hill was the best sight of my life!'

'Rescue at last?'

'That was part of it, but——'

'Look,' she said in a flurry, 'I'd better get back to the house and bring some help. By the look of things a couple of strong men are what you need right now.'

'I'd rather have you, but maybe you're right. You could tell them to fetch the Land Rover, it's got a winch. A long length of timber would be handy as a lever too, and we'll need ropes. Once they can pull the flipping thing away we might be able to get the tractor out of the ditch and up on to firm ground.'

Christine hesitated for a moment. 'Is there anything I can do for you before I go?' Anxiety tinged her tone. 'Anything, just tell me.'

'I'd like to take a rain check on that,' the deep tones were oddly compelling. 'Meantime, just stick around at the house until I get back. We've got a lot of things to talk over, you and I.'

No doubt she thought he wanted to thank her for coming in search of him today. Aloud she murmured, 'There's something I want to tell you too.' She had all but forgotten her motive in seeking Kevin out today in the first place. For some reason she couldn't understand the letter and its contents no longer seemed of prime importance.

If she had travelled swiftly on her way to the gully her journey back to the homestead was equally fast. The fences barring her way were taken with scarcely a second thought and as she sped on she was barely aware of the sheep-dotted slopes that went flashing past her eyes in a shimmer of green.

When she neared the homestead she realised Mrs Hawke must have seen her coming, for the older woman came hurrying down the steps to meet her as Christine rode into the driveway. 'Did you find him? Is he——' She broke off, her face drawn and haggard with anxiety.

'He's all right!' Christine called back, and saw Mrs Hawke's face relax on a great sigh of relief.

'Thank God for that!'

'He is in a spot of bother, though. Seems the tractor

slipped sideways when the bank of the ditch caved in and
he's wedged between the tractor tyre and the bank. I guess
he doesn't dare to try to move the tractor any more for
fear it will——'

'Don't say it! Don't even think of such a thing!' Christine was aware of the unspoken questions forming in the
older woman's mind. Is he really not injured? Is she telling
me the truth? She must be, or she wouldn't be looking so
relieved herself.

'If you could get hold of a couple of men——' Christine
passed on Kevin's message. 'Maybe you could ring up
someone on another farm——'

'No need for that.' Mrs Hawke's gaze was fixed on the
long curve of the driveway where two riders had come into
sight. 'It's Wayne and Ken, they must have left the rodeo
before the others.' To Christine's surprise, Mrs Hawke put
two fingers to her lips and emitted a piercing whistle.
'There! That should bring them here a bit faster!'

Even as she spoke the two shepherds, who had been
ambling along on their horses, galloped to reach the house
and find out what the urgency was about.

Within the space of a few minutes they were joining
Christine and Mrs Hawke. Once they understood the position and need for haste the men hurried away towards the
garages where they got out the Land Rover, threw in ropes
and a long length of timber and took off in the direction of
the hills at the back of the homestead.

'You'll stay, my dear?' There was warmth and affection
in Mrs Hawke's tone. 'What might have happened to Kevin
today if you hadn't gone to find him I don't dare think. If
he'd kept on trying to free the tractor and it had fallen
back on him...'. She shuddered. 'I know he would never
forgive me if I let you slip away before he got back.'

'Thank you. I'll just see to Trooper.' Christine turned her
mount and rode back towards the paddock on the slope.
He only wanted to thank her, of course, and yet—The way
he had looked at her when she had arrived in the gully,
almost one could imagine—but any man trapped as he

was, in danger of losing his life if he made any further effort to free himself, would look pleased as could be at sight of a rescuer on the scene. So don't get carried away and have any mistaken ideas in that direction, Christine girl! she scolded herself.

When she had seen to Trooper she returned the saddle, sheepskin and bridle to the harness shed. Then she took a quick shower and changed into a cool cotton shift. Now it was her turn to watch from the verandah. It seemed to her a long time before she caught sight of a Land Rover coming over the top of the hill. The next moment she realised that Kevin was driving the tractor, so all was well after all.

At the same time as the party reached the driveway the rest of the employees who had spent the day at the rodeo came riding in to join them. As the men talked together Christine gathered that apart from a youth with a bandaged ankle none of the staff of Mata-Rangi appeared to have suffered injury after their hazardous activities of rough-riding and steer-wrestling.

Christine stood a little in the background, achingly aware of Kevin's leather-brown face as he talked with the others. 'If it hadn't been for Christine——' his warm glance went to her and she sent him a shy smile. Shy because there was a certain something in his look, an unspoken message that enclosed them in a private world of their own. Was it her imagination, or did she read a signal in his gaze—'Later'? At least, she told herself wryly, he had approved of something she had done at last.

It wasn't until the evening meal was over and she had helped Mrs Hawke to clear away the dinner dishes that she found an opportunity to see Kevin alone. She knew he was alone because she had taken a peep along the hall a few moments ago to catch a glimpse of him as he smoked a cigarette out on the verandah. Yet now that the moment had arrived she felt a curious diffidence about approaching him. Although she had pretended not to notice all through the meal she had been conscious of his gaze resting on her face and her emotions had alternated between a wild hope and the old familiar feeling of baffled despair.

'Chores all finished?' He had come to seek *her*, and why such a perfectly ordinary remark should fill her with this crazy excitement . . . she seemed to have lost her tongue.

'Yes,' she said at last.

'Well then, come outside with me and take a look at the sunset. It's quite something seen from the rise.'

Without another word she went with him, down the steps that were bathed in a soft pink glow and along a tree-shadowed pathway. It was all like a dream. Surely only in dreams had she heard his voice, soft and low and *loving*, even though the words were conventional enough. 'I owe you a lot for what you did for me today.'

Her face was a pale blur in the gathering gloom of the bush-lined track. 'Oh, it was nothing! I just happened to be the one who was on hand at the time——'

He brushed her protestations aside. 'You were fantastic! But that's not what's on my mind.' They paused together and he drew her close to him. She barely caught the whispered words, 'You did say it?'

'Say . . . what?'

'That "darling", or do you call every man you happen to know that, including Gavin?'

'Gavin?' All at once emotion took over and she forgot to lie and pretend. 'Poor Gavin, he's so good to me, but I—no, I don't call him "darling".'

'That's all I wanted to know!' Very tenderly, his hand beneath her cheek, Kevin turned her face upwards then his lips met hers. His kiss was long and lingering, sweeping away the last of her doubts and pretences. At last he held her a little apart. 'How can I even begin to tell you——' The deep tones broke and he caught her to him. Through the wild rapturous state of her senses she caught the broken words: 'Love you . . . there'll never be anyone else for me, there never was right from the first moment I met you. Only I was fool enough to try to fight against fate and all the time . . . tell me you love me.'

Flushed and tremulous, she said softly, 'All the time I've

been loving you. You must have guessed——'

'Hoped, sweetheart, but you didn't give me much to go on, and then Gavin came into the picture and I took it that everything was settled between you and him. That was when I really went through hell.' He held her at arm's length, proudly, triumphantly. 'Mine . . . all mine. But we've got a lot of straightening out to do. I thought you loathed me.'

A rueful smile played around her lips. 'I did my best to, but it just didn't work, so then I did a lot of pretending. The way you seemed to think about me really made me mad, and I was so sure in my mind that one of these days Andrea and you——'

He shook his head. 'Not in a thousand years, my love. We got off to a bad start, you and I, but man,' his laugh was the laugh of a boy, young and excited and carefree, shot with happiness, 'are we going to make up for it from now on! You'll marry me, say you will, my darling—if you want me?'

'Want you?' It was quite a time before she could concentrate on his words, close against her ear.

'My show-jumper wife? Why did you keep it to yourself, my darling? Why not have told me that you could ride like the wind and jump barbed-wire fences with the best of them? Why the pretence? Why old Brownie and not Trooper?'

'Oh, that!' She laughed with a carefree merriment she hadn't felt for a long time. 'I wasn't just pretending, it was for real, worse luck. I guess I just—lost my nerve for show-jumping.'

He studied her with bright, perceptive eyes. 'There must have been a reason?'

'Oh, there was! You see, last year before I came out to New Zealand I was in hospital for months and months.'

He whistled softly. 'The things I don't know about my bride-to-be!' But he was listening intently. 'Why were you in hospital?'

'I took a fall at a gymkhana, copped a knock on the head

that put me out of action for ages, and then when I got better I had this thing about the high jump, some sort of block in my mind that I couldn't seem to get rid of. When I got the chance of coming out here I thought I'd be able to get the better of it, you know? Riding and all that, seeing I was coming to a country district, but it wasn't any use, the moment I even thought of getting up on Trooper the silly nervous shaking would start. So all I could do was make do with Brownie when it came to riding around the farm with Laurie and hope I'd find some way of getting over the phobia.' Her face was suffused with tenderness. 'I guess in the end it took love to work the miracle. I don't even remember clearing the fences running across the hills I took today on the way to find you. All I knew was that I had to get to you—and fast!'

His tone was thoughtful. 'So that was it.'

'And somehow I've got the feeling I'll never be nervous again,' she finished.

'That's my girl! Living up here with me you'll have lots of chances to prove it.' Elation rang in his tone. 'To have you here with me all the days and,' his tone softened, 'all the nights. You know something, sweetheart, the old Maoris didn't name this place Mata-Rangi for nothing——'

'Fringe of heaven,' she murmured dreamily.

'Right now, though,' he was lifting her hand to his lips, 'we've got things to do. We'll cancel that London air ticket of yours for a start. Then you can tell Laurie and the others that you're not going back to England after all. You'll be moving up the hill instead, living right here at Mata-Rangi.'

A thought occurred to her. 'I was going to send a cable to my mother and stepfather tomorrow——'

'You still can, my love, only it will be to invite them to our wedding.'

Lovely thought. 'What about your parents? Will they mind my living here with them?'

'Good grief, no! They both think the sun shines out of you. Anyway, they've made it plain for a long time now that they're only waiting until I find myself a bride, then they'll move out either down to a smaller place on the flat or into a unit in town—satisfied?'

'I've never been so happy!'

'Me too. From now on it will be plain sailing,' he exulted. 'No more misunderstandings, no more secrets——'

'Except one.' Now that she had arrived at the moment of truth she found it difficult to explain matters. 'I know,' she said breathlessly, 'that when I first arrived here you thought I was a sneaky sort of character?'

'I didn't know you then.'

'But all the same,' she persisted, 'when it came to taking over Glendene——'

'I let my feelings get the better of me about that,' he admitted. 'It took me quite a time to alter that snap decision of mine and come around to thinking that it wasn't your fault that the place had been left to you. In the end I got to thinking that if Laurie could take it and still like you, and he was the one who had the most to lose——'

'What you really thought,' she said teasingly, 'was that somehow I'd had a lot to do with his accepting the position. It wasn't true what you thought, you know.'

'You don't need to tell me, not knowing you as I do now, although how he could give it all up so happily, hand it over lock, stock and barrel to a girl from England whom he'd never seen in his life *and then start working for her*——'

A mischievous smile curved her lips. 'Only he didn't!'

'Didn't?' he queried.

'Lose out, I mean. I had a lawyer in Gisborne transfer the property over to him just a while after I got here, but I couldn't say anything about it to anyone because I knew it would take weeks and weeks to be finalised. All that legal red tape,' her voice was very low, 'and I wanted to show you ... the proof.'

Kevin whistled softly. 'You did that?' He regarded her incredulously. 'Tell me, was Laurie in on this?'

'Yes, he knew, but he was sworn to secrecy, even where

Jan was concerned. *You* were the one I wanted to know. I used to say to myself, if only he knows the truth, if only he doesn't think badly of me after I've gone!'

'What I think about you...' His voice died helplessly away, but the urgency and passion of his kiss told her all she wanted to know.

Much later as they strolled back towards the big house with its dark shelterbelt of trees, stars pricked the blue-darkness of the night sky.

'Home,' Kevin's voice was warm with pride and Christine knew what he meant. 'I wouldn't be surprised,' he said after a moment, 'if that old Maori prophecy about having a bit added on to the house, the room that should have been there when the homestead was first built, doesn't come true after all!'

She glanced up at him to say laughingly, 'A bride who would come to Mata-Rangi from over the sea?'

'A bride who a man could love all his life long. We were meant for each other, you and I,' he told her, and kissed her once again.

When Christine could speak once more she asked: 'What was it that the room was intended for on the old plan?'

'But that's the whole point, my darling,' he said softly. 'What it was meant to be, *is* to be, is a nursery. A whopping big one capable of coping with a growing family, not just one lonely kid on his own.'

'I'll see,' Christine murmured demurely, 'what I can do about it.'

'*We*,' he corrected her gently, then the tenderness and passion of his lips on hers swept everything from her mind.

Harlequin

COLLECTION
EDITIONS OF 1978

**50 great stories
of special beauty
and significance**

$1.25
each novel

In 1976 we introduced the first 100 Harlequin Collections—a selection of titles chosen from our best sellers of the past 20 years. This series, a trip down memory lane, proved how great romantic fiction can be timeless and appealing from generation to generation. The theme of love and romance is eternal, and, when placed in the hands of talented, creative, authors whose true gift lies in their ability to write from the heart, the stories reach a special level of brilliance that the passage of time cannot dim. Like a treasured heirloom, an antique of superb craftsmanship, a beautiful gift from someone loved—these stories too, have a special significance that transcends the ordinary. **$1.25 each novel**

Here are your 1978 Harlequin Collection Editions...

Original Harlequin Romance numbers in brackets

ORDER FORM
Harlequin Reader Service

In U.S.A.
MPO Box 707
Niagara Falls, N.Y. 14302

In Canada
649 Ontario St.,
Stratford, Ontario, N5A 6W2

Please send me the following Harlequin Collection novels. I am enclosing my check or money order for $1.25 for each novel ordered, plus 25¢ to cover postage and handling.

☐ 102	☐ 115	☐ 128	☐ 140
☐ 103	☐ 116	☐ 129	☐ 141
☐ 104	☐ 117	☐ 130	☐ 142
☐ 105	☐ 118	☐ 131	☐ 143
☐ 106	☐ 119	☐ 132	☐ 144
☐ 107	☐ 120	☐ 133	☐ 145
☐ 108	☐ 121	☐ 134	☐ 146
☐ 109	☐ 122	☐ 135	☐ 147
☐ 110	☐ 123	☐ 136	☐ 148
☐ 111	☐ 124	☐ 137	☐ 149
☐ 112	☐ 125	☐ 138	☐ 150
☐ 113	☐ 126	☐ 139	☐ 151
☐ 114	☐ 127		

Number of novels checked @
$1.25 each = $ _____

N.Y. and N.J. residents add
appropriate sales tax $ _____

Postage and handling $ ____.25

TOTAL $ _____

NAME _____
(Please Print)

ADDRESS _____

CITY _____

STATE/PROV. _____

ZIP/POSTAL CODE _____

ABC ROM 2224

Offer expires December 31, 1978

And there's still *more* love in

Harlequin Presents...

Do you have a favorite
Harlequin author?
Then here is an
opportunity you must
not miss!

HARLEQUIN OMNIBUS

Each volume contains
3 full-length compelling
romances by one author.
Almost 600 pages of
the very best in romantic
fiction for only $2.75

A wonderful way to collect
the novels by the Harlequin
writers you love best!